lust

lust

alyssa rose ivy

Cover Design: MaeIDesign and Photography
Interior Designed and Formatted by: Tianne Samson with E.M. Tippetts Book Designs

emtippettsbookdesigns.con

books by
alyssa rose ivy

The Crescent Series
Flight (The Crescent Chronicles #1)
Focus (The Crescent Chronicles #2)
Found (The Crescent Chronicles #3)
First & Forever (The Crescent Chronicles #4)

The Empire Chronicles
Soar (The Empire Chronicles #1)
Search (The Empire Chronicles #2)
Stay (The Empire Chronicles #3)
Savor (The Empire Chronicles #4)

The Allure Chronicles
Seduction's Kiss (The Allure Chronicles #0.5)
Lure (The Allure Chronicles #1)

The Dire Chronicles
Dire (The Dire Wolves Chronicles #1)
Dusk (The Dire Wolves Chronicles #2)

Hazards Series
The Hazards of Skinny Dipping (Hazards)
The Hazards of a One Night Stand (Hazards)
The Hazards of Sex on the Beach (Hazards)
The Hazards of Mistletoe (Hazards)
The Hazards of Sleeping with a Friend (Hazards)

Mixology
Shaken Not Stirred (Mixology)
On The Rocks (Mixology)

Clayton Falls
Derailed (Clayton Falls)
Veer (Clayton Falls)
Wrecked (Clayton Falls)

The Forged Chronicles
Forged in Stone (The Forged Chronicles #1)

www.AlyssaRoseIvy.com
www.facebook.com/AlyssaRoseIvy
twitter.com/AlyssaRoseIvy
New Release Newsletter
AlyssaRoseIvy@gmail.com

preface

I had no real choice. Only one answer was acceptable, yet giving it meant losing everything and anything I cared about. It meant losing Owen, and it meant losing myself.

"Daisy?" Owen looked deep into my eyes.

"I love you." I didn't think, I didn't question. I crushed my lips against his, needing to soak up his taste and feel. He responded immediately, deepening the kiss as he wrapped me up in his arms.

Always and forever. Our promised words swirled through my head. Promised words that couldn't possibly be true. But in that moment it didn't matter. The truth couldn't hurt us. Only time could.

one

daisy

I half expected him to walk away. People are good at promising things. The promise is the easy part. Keeping the promise takes more work. Yet there he was, driving us from Arizona to New Orleans in a borrowed car that had seen better days. Owen had talked to a friend of a friend he knew in the area. I didn't have any other ideas, and at least he wasn't manipulating anyone to get it. I'd had the urge. A small one I was able to dampen by walking away, but it was there, and that reality scared me. It was another reminder that I was no longer completely human.

"You okay?" Owen put a hand on my leg. I was already used to his touch. I wasn't sure how I'd managed so many years without it. I also wasn't sure how I could ever manage without it in the future.

I wanted to pretend nothing had changed, that I wasn't going to lose my ability to feel, but that crazy thought seemed more and more possible. My emotions were going haywire, and more often than not, I didn't feel like myself.

"Okay enough." I kept my voice level even though I felt anything but calm. If I didn't know about the Allure essence I'd have assumed I was having a hormonal imbalance. These mood swings made my PMS complaints seem like a joke.

"That's not good enough." He took his eyes off the road long enough to give me a worried once over.

"Would you prefer I lied?" I didn't want to be rude to him. I wanted to be all sugar and light, but I couldn't be. Not now.

"No, I want you to relax."

"Relax? I just found out my life as I know it is over."

"It's been over for years." His voice was flat, but I knew it wasn't indifference. He was trying to reign in his true feelings as much as I was.

"True." A smile slipped out despite my sour mood. Owen was good at making that happen.

"We're going to fix this. We're going to fix everything. And after that we're going to work on us." He squeezed my thigh lightly. There was nothing overtly sexual about the action, but that's exactly where my thoughts begged to go. I'd only had a small taste of him. I wanted more. I wanted more of everything, in bed and out.

"Work on us?" I raised an eyebrow. "I wasn't aware there was anything to fix." Everything causing our problems was external, or in my case internal, but having nothing to do with my true thoughts or feelings about him. We were solid.

"That came out wrong." A panicked look crossed his face. "There is nothing about us to fix. I mean focus on us."

"Gotcha." I smiled again. His concern over upsetting me

was cute.

"We deserve some quality time."

"I still can't believe I'm sitting next to you." I relaxed against the seat. Dingy or not, the car was taking us toward help. We needed any of it we could get.

"That makes two of us." He took my hand in his. "The thing is though; there is nowhere else I'd want to be."

"You'd rather be flying." I wasn't sure why I kept trying to sabotage things, but my emotions didn't give me a choice. They changed and pushed me to say things I didn't want to mean. But I did mean them, even if another voice inside of me was screaming that I shouldn't.

"Ok. I'd rather be flying—with you. Or in bed with you for that matter."

My body warmed thinking about all the things I wanted to do in bed with him. "I'm with you there."

"Maybe that's what you need, huh?" He winked.

"You think you can cure my stress with sex?" As wonderful and enticing of a thought as it was, my luck wasn't that good.

"I know I can. If we weren't in a rush…"

"If we were in a rush we could have flown." I closed my eyes and imagined the sensation of flying. The wind all around us. The feel of his body pressed against mine.

"We needed some time before we got there."

"We did." I squeezed his hand. "I'm sorry. This isn't me. I'm not obnoxious and mean."

"I know. I know who you are." There wasn't a hint of wavering in his voice. He still saw the real me, even if it was getting more and more buried by the minute.

"Or who I was… ugh."

"You are still you. We'll get rid of the other stuff." He changed lanes to pass a slow moving car.

"Are you always this optimistic?"

He laughed. "No. I'm usually considered the opposite. My friends give me a hard time about my unrelenting realism."

"Then how can you be so confident right now?" I envied his confidence. I wondered where I'd have been without him. Probably in a ditch waiting out the last days of my humanity.

He slowed down and moved into the exit lane.

"What are you doing?"

"I'm going to remind you of where my confidence comes from."

"Owen…" Needing time together or not, we had to move. Who knew when the Allure part of me would fully take over? I shivered. I couldn't stomach the thought of losing the ability to feel, especially since it meant losing my feelings for Owen. I refused to accept that.

"Yes, Daisy?" He pulled off at the next exit.

"What are you doing?" I looked out at the dark night sky.

"You already asked that question, and I answered."

I thought over his answer. Maybe the stop would be one I wanted. One I needed.

He parked the car in a gas station parking lot. "Come on. Grab your purse, we're leaving the car."

"Okay." I didn't question him. Despite everything, I trusted Owen completely. I assumed he would take care of making sure the owner got the car back. He wasn't like Violet and the guys. He wasn't an Allure. Not like me.

By the time he met me on my side of the car he already had his shirt off. I'd been right. We were going for a flight. I waited anxiously as he moved behind me. His arms wrapped around my waist, and my stomach lurched the way it always did when he took off, but soon it settled down. I knew I was in good hands.

I kept my eyes open as we soared through the night sky. The wind was cold and a stark contrast to Owen's warm body pressed against mine. His body was hard, but it gave me comfort like nothing else could ever give.

After a few minutes, we landed in a dense forest, and I stumbled away from him. I took in his muscular chest, his large black wings, and I couldn't wait any longer. I reached out for him. Before my hands could make contact he had me in his arms again. His lips pressed against mine, and he quickly demanded access to my mouth. I gladly let him in, reveling in his taste as he continued to deepen the kiss. His hand slipped underneath the front of my shirt, and I ran my hand up and down the muscular planes of his chest. With my other hand I touched his back, disappointed to find his wings gone, but his roving hands and lips made my disappointment melt away.

"I need you," he whispered against my ear.

"You have me." That much was true. It would always be true.

"Here?" He pulled away enough to lock eyes with me.

"Anywhere." To let him know I wasn't kidding, I unbuttoned his jeans.

He chuckled. "Glad I'm not the only one."

"This has never been one sided." I returned my lips to his, needing more.

He stepped out of his jeans and boxers all the while removing my jeans.

He unclasped and discarded my bra and his lips immediately went to my breast. I closed my eyes and focused on the sensation. I moaned, surprised when he pulled us both to the ground.

I lay on top of him with only my underwear separating me from what I wanted. What I needed. "Thanks for taking the brunt of the ground."

"You like my excuse to get you on top?" He grinned. "We'll make the next time romantic." He put his hand underneath the waist band of my underwear.

I took a condom from my bag and handed it to him. He'd be faster. "You didn't need an excuse."

He watched me expectedly as I slowly eased him inside of me.

He groaned. "Daisy."

I continued to move on top of him, letting all of my worries and fears disappear. This was real. This was feeling. It wasn't just physical, it was emotional and mental. It was everything.

"You feel that?" he said between heavy breaths.

"Yes." I felt everything.

"Remember this." His eyes locked on mine, relaying the same message as his words.

I nodded, unable to speak as I struggled to hold myself together.

With no warning he flipped us over so I was underneath. He took control, moving in hard and deep thrusts. I closed my eyes, soaking up every feeling and sensation I could. The feel of his skin, his lips, and the way he made me feel complete.

"Remember this. Remember what it feels like to be with

me."

"I will." I promised, even though I knew I shouldn't. In that moment I believed it though. I believed I was still in control of my destiny.

"I promise to never let you forget."

I opened my eyes, wanting to watch his pleasure as I experienced my own. Our bodies moved in perfect sync, as he made it harder and harder for me to stay in control. I bit down on my lip to stay quiet.

"We're alone, Daisy. You don't have to hold back." He ran his lips down my neck.

I listened, calling out his name as he rocked me to my core and brought me to a level of pleasure I'd never been before. The first few times had been great, but this was different. There was an intensity and connection I'd have never believed could exist.

"Daisy," he groaned, as he sped up his movements. I was getting close, and I urged him on, wrapping my legs up around his body.

"Owen!" I called out his name as he pushed me over the edge. My eyes closed without conscious thought, it was the only way to handle the incredible sensations running through my body.

He shuddered and lay down on top of me. Neither of us said anything for a moment. We were both sweaty and out of breath, and perfect. The moment was perfect.

"Hope your back is okay." He picked his head up to look at me.

I ignored the dull ache in my back. "Totally worth it."

He smiled before brushing his lips against mine. "You are amazing."

"So are you." I ran my hand down his back.

"You make me reckless." He cupped my face with his hand.

"You make me desperate."

"Desperate in a good way I hope."

"Desperate in the best way." I pulled his lips to mine again.

He laughed against my lips. "I want to lie here with you forever."

"I may have downplayed the whole back in the dirt thing." It felt fine in the heat of the passion, but now it was starting to get old.

He slipped his arms under me. "I'll make it up to you."

"It's already made up."

"Are you up for flying the rest of the way there?" He played with a few tendrils of my hair.

"Once I get dressed." I kissed his shoulder. I wanted to get in every kiss I could.

"You mean you don't want to fly naked with me?" he teased.

"If we were landing in a place as secluded as this sure, but something tells me someone might see us when we land in New Orleans."

"That something is right."

"You'll stay with me?" I didn't want to sound needy, but that's exactly how I felt. For the first time all day my emotions legitimately felt like mine. I felt euphoric yet terrified. The warring emotions were real and true, and that made the terror worth it.

"I'm never leaving your side." He looked deep into my eyes. "Never."

I nodded. "Good."

He kissed me lightly. "You better get used to me, Daisy. I'm not going anywhere."

"I was hoping you'd say that." I pulled him down against me again. We could stand to wait another minute before getting dressed.

two

owen

I never expected to return to New Orleans with a girlfriend, especially not one like Daisy, but as I closed in on my hometown, holding Daisy's body firmly in my arms, there was no question that I was doing exactly that.

She was silent during the flight, but that wasn't surprising considering how high we were in the air and the strong wind. She wasn't screaming, so I took that as a win.

"We're almost there." I broke the silence in order to give her warning. I was using the last airborne minutes to prepare for the craziness. She deserved to have the same opportunity.

"I'm going to be sick," she mumbled. Even over the wind my hearing was good enough to pick it up.

"Because of the altitude?" She'd never had a problem flying with me before.

"Not at all."

"It's going to be fine. I'll be with you the whole time."

"Promise?"

"Promise." I didn't plan to ever break a promise to her.

"I'm holding you to it."

"I know." I adjusted her slightly as I began our descent.

It was dark, but early enough in the evening I needed to be careful not to be spotted. Occasionally it happened, but you couldn't take chances too often. I landed in the shadows around back of the Crescent City Hotel. I hoped Levi was still at work. The alternative was to show up at his house, and although I was sure he and Allie wouldn't care, it might make the situation even more awkward for Daisy. The Society chambers were intimidating, but I hoped it would be easier for her. She seemed better at focusing on the less personal side of things. Either way, we needed answers, and Levi was the only place to start.

I landed, and Daisy stumbled out of my arms. She straightened out her clothes and ran a hand through her windblown hair. She pulled a stick out of it. That wasn't from the wind. I pulled out a leaf and laughed.

"You think this is funny?" She put a hand on her hip.

"Yes, it's funny only because I still can't really believe we did that."

"You started it."

"I'm quite aware of that." I took her hand in mine.

"Not that I'm complaining."

"Good. I hope to never hear complaints about that." I pulled her against me.

"I wouldn't worry."

I tensed when I heard footsteps. It was only a couple of tourists. They were staring at us. What was their problem?

"You should probably put your shirt on." She nudged me.

"I suppose that would make us look less conspicuous."

"Or at least put it in on if we're going to spend more time in this alley. Otherwise it looks like we're about to do unsavory things."

"Unsavory? I thought we already did those. Unless you want a repeat." I raised an eyebrow.

"As much as I want to put off talking to Levi, we need to do this."

"We do." I pulled on my t-shirt. "Ready?"

"I don't have another choice."

"No, you don't."

She seemed slightly surprised by my candor. I always wanted to be open and honest with her, which meant being realistic about what was happening.

I led her around to the front of the building, keeping her hand firmly covered by mine. She squeezed my hand as we walked through the doors. I squeezed back.

"Good evening and welcome to the Crescent City Hotel." A bellboy I'd never seen before greeted us as we stepped into the air-conditioned lobby.

"Thanks," Daisy mumbled.

He grinned at her. "If there is anything I can do to make your visit more pleasurable, please let me know."

"Thanks." She looked away.

"Really, I would be happy to help you with any of your needs." He leaned toward her.

"I'm fine."

"How about a tour of the Quarter? I get off in an hour."

"Sorry, not interested."

"Come on, I don't bite."

She recoiled, and I knew she had to be thinking about the vampires.

I put an arm around her. "You won't be speaking to her again."

"Can I at least get your number?" He ignored me.

"What part of 'you won't be speaking to her' don't you understand?" I stepped toward him.

He moved back. "Whoa, man. It's a free country. You don't own her."

"He doesn't own me, but we're together. That means I'm not interested." She turned and started walking away. I led us toward the elevator. I looked over my shoulder and glared at the bellboy one last time to make sure he got the message.

"Thanks for the help back there." Daisy leaned back against the wall of the elevator. "I like the whole jealous thing on you."

"How can you stand that attention?" I moved next to her.

"I ignore it mostly. It wasn't as bad before I returned to New Orleans, and then I was only focused on one thing, finding you."

My heart soared yet again, as it did every time she mentioned how hard she'd searched for me. It meant nothing was one sided. She'd been as affected by the long ago kiss as I was.

I led us onto the elevator as soon as it arrived. After inserting my key, we started moving toward the basement floor of the hotel that shouldn't have even existed.

The elevator doors opened into darkness. There was enough light that my night vision worked, but I doubted Daisy's had gotten that strong.

"Don't let go of me." She leaned heavily into my side.

"Not planning on it. I'm jealous, remember."

She laughed. "See, I knew the Allure would be good for

something."

"We're getting rid of it."

"Obviously."

I led us right to Levi's office, the same office that had once been his father's. I knocked.

"Yes?" His familiar voice called out.

I opened the door a crack. "Got a minute?"

The door flew open. "You never called me back."

"We decided to drop by unannounced." Daisy surprised me by talking.

Levi laughed. "And I see you two found each other."

"Yes." I tightened my hold on her. "Which is why we need your help."

"My help?" His eyes widened. "I don't believe you've ever asked for my help, Owen."

"And I hope I don't have to again, but we need it now."

"Come in." He gestured for us to enter his office.

Nothing had changed inside the surprisingly small space. The same massive wood desk took up most of the room, with two visitor chairs set in front of it. Despite his position as king, Levi's office was one of the smallest. Still, the room was comfortable, and he'd managed to put his mark on it. The biggest ones were the pictures of his family.

Daisy pointed to the photo of Allie. "Does she mind that you work late?"

He nodded. "Yes."

"Honest." Daisy nodded with approval.

"She knows I only do it when I have to. I try not to bring work home."

"Is that possible? I mean you are the king."

"Someone spilled the beans I see." He looked at me.

"Yeah… I had no idea I'd been rude to royalty. Sorry about that." She looked down.

"You're not really sorry."

"No." She met his eyes again. "But I do feel for your wife."

"I'll be sure to pass on the concern, but as I can't go home until we finish talking and I send another few emails, let's do this." He gestured for us to take the two chairs in front of his desk before he settled into his own chair. I pulled out one chair for Daisy, and then sat down in the other.

"I'm not sure where to start." The story was a crazy one.

"I'd love to know how you two found each other, but my guess is that isn't really why you need my help." He rested his hands on his desk. Sometimes he looked so much like his father it was eerie. He had the same powerful gaze, and he exuded the confidence and strength that came with being king.

I went for the punch line. "The Allures are still around."

"What?" Levi sat up in a flash.

"They are back." I slightly reworded my comment.

"Your friends." He turned to Daisy. "That's what they were." Understanding crossed his face.

She nodded. "Yes."

"Are they threatening you? Is that why you need help? You need Society protection?" Levi was sitting up watching our every move. He had moved into action mode.

She shook her head. "Nothing that easy."

He caught my eye. "That would be easier?"

"You remember how I first met her. She'd been given a paste—concocted by a local witch."

"Yes. I remember. Halloween night. Vampires."

"I believed Mayanne had gotten rid of all the effects from

17

the paste, but she hadn't." I glanced over my shoulder at the closed door. "There was an Allure essence in the paste."

"What?" Levi startled. "How is that possible?"

"It is..." Daisy sighed.

"So you need help extracting it?"

"Yes, and fast." I put a hand on Daisy's back. I could tell she was getting frustrated.

"Did the Allures give you a timeline?"

"Not exactly." Daisy looked at me, and I nodded. "If we can't get rid of it, I will become an Allure."

"Become one?" He looked between us.

We both nodded. "And it means she will no longer feel." A chill ran through me. "That can't happen." It wasn't an option. Levi needed to know I wasn't giving up. I'd do anything to stop the change.

"How much time are we talking?"

"Not long." Daisy sighed. "I already feel the change happening. Just ask Owen, I'm a basket case. I'm not me anymore."

"Yes, you are." I ran my hand up and down her back. "You are still you." She was moody, but that didn't mean her core personality had changed.

"I can handle the truth, Owen. You don't have to pretend."

"I'm not pretending." She slumped down further in her chair.

She shook her head. "Forget it then. Let's get back to discussing the important things."

I took Daisy's hand. "The only clue we have is a place called Energo. Ever heard of it?"

"Energo?" he asked. "Is it a town?"

"I have no clue. The witch said we wouldn't find it on our

maps, but it has to be on The Society ones."

Levi nodded. "Everything exists on our maps." He turned back to his laptop. "Let me finish one more email, and then we can go back to my house. I have all the old documents there now." He nodded, which meant he'd made a plan.

Last time I'd been in town the maps were in the Society safe. I'd been banking on the process being easy. "Why did you move them?" There was no place safer than The Society chambers. The security was the best around.

"Security reasons," Levi was being purposely vague. I hoped it wasn't out of a lack of trust for either of us. It was strange to be out of the loop on anything Society related, but that's what happens when you take a break for a few months.

"Wait, we are going back to your house?" Daisy's eyes widened.

"Yes." Levi typed something on his keyboard before closing his laptop. "Is there a problem with that?"

"You should get permission from your wife." She pointed to Allie's picture.

"You are very concerned about her." He stood up.

"I know getting on her bad side isn't going to help."

"I'll call, but I promise she won't care. She'll be excited about Owen's return."

"I haven't returned," I quickly disputed. "At least not until we fix this." I missed my job and my friends and family, but I couldn't even think about returning until we figured out how to stop the change.

"I understand. We will work fast. I need you here." Levi picked up his phone. "Give me a second."

We waited while he called Allie. I knew Levi was right, she wouldn't care at all about him bringing us back. Well, not

19

if he warned her.

Daisy glanced around Levi's office nervously. I squeezed her hand. "It's going to be fine."

"I know."

"You're nervous," I whispered, brushing my lips against her ear.

"Just anxious to find out more." She crossed her legs.

"Allie is really nice."

"I don't doubt that."

"Just know I'll be with you the whole time."

"And I appreciate that." She smiled in a forced way.

"Because I want to be, not because I have to be."

"And I *really* appreciate that." Her smile was more genuine this time.

"If all else fails, we sneak off and have sex. That steadies you."

She hit my arm playfully. "Owen."

"Yes, Daisy?" I would never get tired of hearing her say my name, even if she was saying it because she was annoyed.

"Cool it."

"What? You were in such a good mood after that."

"Of course I was. How could I not be in a good mood? You were too."

"As you said, how could I not be?"

"Uh, you two done talking about sex?" Levi rubbed the back of his neck.

I laughed, and Daisy looked horrified.

"Don't worry." He touched her arm gently. "I'm getting Owen back for all the crap he gave me."

"Okay…" Daisy looked toward the door. "How are we getting there?"

"Driving." Levi spun his keys in his hand. "But by the question I assume you are a fan of flight?"

Daisy nodded. "I am, but a car is good too."

I smiled. "It takes longer to drive, but we can't fly around the city all the time."

"Gotcha."

Levi led the way back to the elevator. I took Daisy's hand in mine. She leaned into my side. I loved knowing I brought her comfort. She may have lost confidence, but I hadn't. We would find a way to reverse the change. I refused to accept any other outcome.

three

daisy

I stared out the window as Levi drove us up St. Charles Avenue. Despite the insanity of the situation, I couldn't help but marvel at the beautiful homes that lined St. Charles Avenue. Complete with large front porches, many with columns and surrounded by live oak trees with hanging moss, the area was gorgeous. If the city wasn't home to some of my worst nightmares, I would have said it was my favorite. Maybe meeting Owen there made up for all that. Or it would if I got to stay with him.

"Is it too hot back there?" Levi glanced over his shoulder to where I sat. I'd refused to sit up front, much to Owen's annoyance. When he'd gotten ready to slide into the back, Levi had promptly told him he wasn't playing chauffeur. Owen sat right down in the passenger seat. It was strange watching him answer to someone else. I knew Levi was king, but that didn't make it seem any more normal.

"No, it's fine," I assured him. The AC was actually so high

it was making me cold.

"Ok, just checking. You seemed hot."

"Can you tell that I'm sweating?"

"Yes." Levi smiled at me in the rearview mirror.

"Darn heightened senses."

He laughed. "My guess is you have some interesting talents of your own now."

I groaned. "Don't remind me."

"But they won't work on your boy, here." He tapped the back of Owen's seat.

"I know. At least I know he likes me for me." Otherwise I'd have been constantly worried it was all the Allure. It was still hard to believe he was that into me. Owen was the kind of guy who could have had any girl he wanted.

"I more than like you." Owen turned around and smiled.

I smiled in return. Despite everything, it was nice to know my feelings were reciprocated.

"You two need to mellow out."

"Like you are one to talk." Owen stiffened.

"And you let me have it when I did the same thing. Fair is fair." Levi laughed. He was different than I expected. He had more of a sense of humor than he'd shown me in our first few meetings. I assumed it was because I was with Owen. That somehow moved me into the friend camp instead of unknown potential enemy. "Did you get to enjoy much of the city the last time you were here?"

"Some, but not enough." Even my leisurely exploration had gotten me in trouble last time.

"Let's get all this settled, and then we'll give you a proper tour." He said proper in a way that accentuated his slight southern accent. Owen's was a little bit more pronounced—

and sexier.

"Your wife is really okay with us coming back with you?" I didn't want to make a bad impression on the queen.

"Yes. Surprised, but happy. She apologized in advance that she didn't make enough dinner."

"We won't take up too much of your time. We can leave and let you two enjoy the rest of the evening."

"We have a kid," he said casually.

"So?" I waited for the punch line. What was his point?

"So how much do you think we'll be enjoying the evening?"

I laughed. "Good point. But don't they go to bed soon?"

"He should be in bed already, I'm only emphasizing that you aren't interrupting anything."

"How's the little one anyway?" Owen turned in his seat.

"Cute and annoying at the same time."

"He's only acting tough." Owen turned around. "You should see him when he's in dad mode."

I smiled. "Having kids can change a man."

"And a woman." Levi laughed quietly. "Allie has changed."

"She's probably much busier." Being queen likely wasn't all fun and games.

"She is. Finding a work-life balance has taken her some time."

"Allie works?" I didn't hide my surprise. "But she's the queen."

"You don't know Allie yet." Owen turned to me again. "She's slowed down on work and school since becoming a mom, but my guess is that's temporary. When she's dedicated to something, you had better hope you are not on the opposing side."

"I've learned that the hard way." Levi turned onto a beautiful tree lined street.

I took several deep breaths. I could do this. Meeting the queen couldn't be any worse than meeting the king, even if I'd already met him before I knew who he was.

Owen turned around. "You okay?"

"Fine." I gritted my teeth. I wished he realized that asking me if I was okay made it worse. I didn't need any more attention drawn to me.

I looked out the window again to avoid meeting his gaze. Levi turned into a stone, circular driveway and stopped in front of a giant white house. Tall columns spanned up to both levels of the house, while large southern oaks and a magnolia tree dominated the perfectly manicured yard.

I was so busy staring that Levi nearly gave me a heart attack when he opened my door.

He must have noticed my shocked expression, because he laughed. "Sorry to startle you."

"Nice house."

He smiled. "Thanks." He held out a hand. I awkwardly accepted it.

We walked around the car, and I met up with Owen. He quickly scooped my hand up in his. Levi walked up to the wrap around porch, and we followed. Before he could get his key in the lock, the door was thrown open. A large golden retriever ran out on the porch and jumped on Levi.

"Get down, Sally!" Levi yelled at the dog.

"Don't yell at her!" A brunette walked out onto the porch. She was wearing jeans and a t-shirt with her hair tied up in a knot on the top of her head, but she had this ethereal beauty that made it look like she would fit more on a runway than a home—even one as grand as this one. I knew at once it was the queen, Allie.

"I wouldn't yell if she didn't jump up on people," Levi grumbled.

Allie ignored her husband and walked over to me with her hand outstretched. "You must be Daisy."

"Yes, hi. Nice to meet you." I accepted her firm handshake.

"Come right in. Sorry about the dog." She smiled apologetically.

"It's fine. I grew up with two labs."

"Oh, those are great dogs too." She gestured for me to walk inside.

I listened, assuming Owen would follow us in.

I looked around at the tall ceilings and beautifully refinished hardwood floors. "You have a lovely home." Try amazing. I'd never been in a place quite like it before.

"It's a mess." She bent down and picked up a truck. "I'm sorry. I finally got the little guy down and ran out of time to clean up."

"Don't you guys have maids?" I regretted the words once they were out. I didn't want to make her uncomfortable.

She smiled. "We have a house cleaner, but only once a week. Otherwise it's up to me to pick up after everyone."

"I clean too." Levi walked over and kissed her on the cheek.

She smiled. "Occasionally."

"Hey, you've been complaining we never have company. I brought you company."

"With no notice. I would have hired a sitter and had dinner catered."

"Allie isn't much of a cook," Owen laughed.

Allie nudged Levi. "I'm getting better. Right?"

He smiled. "You are fantastic, babe. No question about it."

"Do you want to be in trouble?" She narrowed her eyes.

"What?" He held up his hands as if in defense. "I was being honest. You're a great cook."

"I heard some sarcasm there." She flushed.

"Keep up with this over sensitive stuff, and I'm going to worry you are pregnant again."

She swatted at him. "If we didn't have company you'd be regretting those words."

"And my guess is I'll be regretting them after they leave." He pulled her into his arms. "Have I told you lately that I love you?"

"Sweet talk isn't going to work."

"It won't?" He rested his forehead against hers. "Even if it's really sweet?"

Allie shook her head. "And on that note, let's move into the living room. I'm sure our guests would like to get on with the evening."

Allie and Levi walked through a large archway. I pulled Owen back. "Are they always like this?" I whispered.

He laughed. "Most of the time. Entertaining couple, aren't they?"

"You could say that." I followed them into the living room.

I took a seat on a beige couch, glad when Owen sat down next to me. Allie and Levi sat down across from us on a loveseat.

"Levi didn't get a chance to tell me to what I owed the pleasure of your company, Owen. My guess is this is more than a purely social visit?" She crossed her legs.

"We need to take a look at some maps. We have to find a place."

"A place? Very descriptive." She huffed.

"Do you know anything about the Allures?" I asked.

"I've read about them. They are an ancient mythical creature if I'm correct."

"Ancient yes, but not mythical." Owen put a hand on my leg.

"Wait, you've seen them?" Allie sat up.

"Daisy's got one in her." Levi didn't move an inch when he spoke.

"Uh, what does he mean?" She watched me warily.

"Oh, I ate one for breakfast." I needed to lighten the mood.

Allie laughed. "Funny."

"Glad you figured out it was a joke."

She laughed again. "I'm not that gullible, but what is Levi talking about?"

"Short story is she was given a magic paste that apparently had Allure essence in it. She'll fully become one if we don't stop it." Levi stood up. "I'll pull out the maps. Owen, want to join me?"

He wasn't really asking, and Owen stood right up. He glanced down at me. "We'll be right back.

"Please find something," I pleaded.

"I'll do my best."

I watched as they walked out of the room.

"Can I get you something to drink?" Allie snapped me out of my daze. "I know I should be asking how you are, but I already know you can't be doing great. A drink is the only thing I can think to offer."

"You are nothing like I expected."

"What did you expect?" She walked over and sat down next to me.

"A pampered princess type girl."

"Sorry to disappoint you." Her eyes twinkled.

"About that drink you offered?"

"My guess is you need something strong."

"As strong as you've got."

"Come with me." She led the way into the next room and stopped in front of a large mahogany bar. "Pick your poison." She gestured to a row of top shelf liquors.

"Vodka." I didn't drink much liquor, but I preferred Vodka.

"Neat?"

"That works." I didn't plan to drink much, so I wanted to be easy.

She poured two glasses and handed me one.

"To the boys finding what you need on the maps." She lightly tapped her glass against mine.

"Cheers." I sipped the strong liquor and welcomed the burn as it went down my throat.

Allie took a sip. "A few years ago I wouldn't have had this."

"You've changed your drink preferences?" I asked. The whole situation was strange. Having drinks with a queen was never in my plans.

"Yes. I'm not sure how much of that comes from being queen versus being a mom."

I laughed. "My guess is both contribute."

"So you and Owen, huh?" She sipped her vodka again.

"Yup, me and Owen."

"Other than the whole Allure thing, are you doing well?"

"I'm crazy about him."

"And the sex?"

I coughed on my drink.

She held out a hand. "Sorry, had to ask." She laughed. "I'm nosier than I used to be."

Why not be honest? "It's great."

"He seems happy. Stressed but happy."

"I'd say that sums me up, but my emotions aren't that simple anymore."

"Are you like an Allure? I read something about them being able to manipulate feelings."

"I can somewhat. I'm trying to avoid it."

"The worst part about being a human in this paranormal world is that I'm susceptible to everything while Levi isn't. At least my kids will be immune."

"Will all of them be Pteron?" I couldn't imagine having kids that weren't human. Then again I couldn't imagine not being human myself but that was already starting to happen.

"Yes. That gene is dominant."

"What's that like? Having kids that have wings?"

"You're changing the subject." She swirled around the liquor in her glass.

"I am." There was no reason to pretend otherwise.

"Sneaky."

"I am legitimately curious."

"It's different, but I knew what I was getting into. My guess is it's going to be more of a challenge as they get older." She glanced over her shoulder, and I assumed she was checking to make sure Levi wasn't listening. "I'm worried they'll look down on me, or I'll feel left out because I can't fly."

"That would be hard." I didn't beat around the bush. She hadn't with me, so I would give her the same courtesy.

"Like I said, I don't know what changed my liquor preference more." She took another sip.

"I'm sorry for this unexpected visit."

"It's fine. Owen is like family. I'm surprised Levi even called in advance to let me know."

"I made him." It was the least we could do.

She smiled. "Why am I not surprised?"

"Men don't think about things like that."

"No, they don't. And to be honest some women don't either."

"Yes, I'll agree there." I'd definitely met my fair share of those.

"How are you feeling?" She leaned back against the bar. "

"Emotionally I'm a mess, but physically I'm feeling normal enough."

"I know you've got to be terrified, but we're going to figure this out."

"If it's possible."

"You know it is. Otherwise you wouldn't be here." She gave me a knowing look.

"Ladies?" Levi called from the doorway. "Starting without us?" He took Allie's glass and sipped it. "You're drinking vodka now?"

She shrugged. "There are worse things."

"Find anything?" Allie and Levi's banter was cute and all, but I didn't have time to waste.

"Yes and no." Owen walked over with a roll of paper under his arms.

"Are those the maps?"

"Yes. I want to show you something." He walked toward the kitchen and laid out the map on the table. "This is the map of all known cities and locations in the world."

"Where's Energo?" I stood next to him.

"That's the thing." He tapped the map. "It's not on here."

"Or this one." Levi rolled out another map next to it.

"So how does any of this help us?" I could feel my frustration rising along with panic.

"Owen doesn't think Kalisa was lying about Energo." Levi leaned a land on the table.

"Why would she have lied? What could she have possibly gained by that?" I agreed with his assessment, but that didn't mean it helped us at all.

"If she's telling the truth, then there are only two possibilities." Levi tapped the maps.

"And they are?" I was growing increasingly inpatient.

"Either Energo is another name for a place."

"Or?"

Levi rolled the maps back up. "Or it doesn't exist in our world as we know it."

"Uh... if it doesn't exist in our world, where does it exist?" Allie scrunched up her forehead.

"Allie, do you still have those books you borrowed from my grandma? The ones about all the ancient creatures?"

Allie put a hand under her chin. "No. Georgina made me return them in less than forty-eight hours."

"Georgina?" I asked.

"My grandma, don't ask." Levi shook his head.

"Wait, do you think the places described in those books are real then?" Allie leaned forward.

"The Allures are still around…"

"Does this mean we're paying a visit to Georgina?" Owen's eyes brightened.

"Yes." Levi nodded. "But she's out at the country home. It's going to be a drive."

"Doesn't matter." Owen grabbed my hand. "I'm not going to pretend Georgina is the easiest person to get along with, but if anyone is going to be able to help, it's her."

"Then why didn't we go to her first?" I asked what I thought was an obvious question.

Levi laughed. "Because no one just goes to Georgina, except for family, and even we're careful. The matriarch of our familiar is intense."

"But most of that is an act." Allie took my empty glass from me. "She's more bark than bite unless you get on her bad side. If you do that, well, then you're in serious trouble."

"But you think she'll help us?" I clasped my hands together.

"She's always had a soft spot for Owen." Levi grinned. "Now if this was Jared it would be another story."

"Who's Jared?" I asked.

"No one you need to know." Owen linked his arm with mine.

"He's their other best friend." Allie put a hand on her hip. "But you really don't need to worry about him yet. I'm sure you'll meet him eventually."

"Maybe someday." Owen pulled me toward the door.

I decided not to press him. I had bigger things to worry about. Like meeting Levi's grandmother. She couldn't be that scary, could she?

four

owen

I was glad that Daisy didn't know all the stories about Georgina. She was going to have to meet her anyway, so there was no reason to needlessly stress her out. Usually I was all about preparing someone for an experience, but there was too much going on. I wanted to keep things as calm as possible.

"You can take a nap if you want." I turned from the front seat to watch her in the back. She'd insisted on sitting in the back again. Levi had offered to chauffer us, but Daisy was adamant he didn't. She seemed upset that we'd somehow be putting him out.

"I'm fine." She looked out the window.

"Please stop saying that."

"Why? What do you want me to say?"

"Anything but fine. Fine is just another way of saying bad."

"That's not true."

"Would you two stop arguing?" Levi watched me out of the corner of his eye. "This is supposed to be a peaceful job."

"Who said it was going to be peaceful?" Daisy snapped.

The expression that followed her words said it all. She was horrified. "Sorry."

Levi laughed. "And I thought Allie was the only one who would ever talk back to me."

"She probably hates me."

"Why?"

"You were home for less than an hour, you barely saw her, and now you're leaving again."

"She understands." Levi backed out of the driveway. "You worry a lot about my wife."

"It's more like redirected guilt."

"Don't feel guilty. Owen knows I'd do anything for him, plus this is Society business."

"Why?" Daisy sat forward in her seat. "How is this Society business?"

"Because the Allures aren't supposed to be here. If they are, I need to know about it, and I have to make sure humans aren't being turned into them left and right."

"I doubt that's the case." I shifted in my seat. I wanted to get into the back with her. "Taking down an Allure couldn't have been easy for the witch to do, and from what I understand, not all humans could have been able to handle the essence."

"Oh, Daisy is special then?" Levi raised an eyebrow.

"Yes, but for more reasons than that."

"Sweet." He smiled.

We settled into a comfortable silence as we drove on I-10 heading toward the country.

Daisy broke the silence. "How much farther is it?" Her voice was strained, and I could tell she was trying to stay polite.

"Not much farther."

"And you don't think she's going to mind us showing up at night like this?"

"She'll mind."

"Then why are we doing it?" Daisy threw up her hands.

"Because she'll forgive us when she finds out why we're there. You guys keep saying time is of the essence. Waiting until morning seemed like a mistake." He sped up to pass a slow moving truck.

"You think she'll give us time to explain?" Daisy fidgeted in her seat.

"I'm the king. Even Georgina has to accept that."

I chuckled. "Good luck with that approach, man."

"Let me do the talking." Levi changed lanes and took an exit, and we turned onto a country road.

"I was planning on it." Daisy folded her hands in her lap. "I'm more than happy to wait in the car even."

"You're coming in. Like I said, she'll forgive the unannounced visit if she knows it's for a reason."

"I hope you're right." Daisy leaned back against the tan leather seat.

The sky was pitch black when Levi pulled into the long drive leading up to Georgina's plantation home. The drive was surrounded by a magnificent alley of oaks that led the way to a beautiful, old home situated on several acres of land. Despite the distance from New Orleans, I understood why they'd moved out there. Maybe I could find a place like this where Daisy and I could stay close enough that I could work for Levi, but we could still get away from it all. I'd stopped thinking about my future in terms of just me. I was now viewing it as a joint venture, and I liked it.

I met Daisy as soon as she opened the door, and I held out my hand. I knew she liked to do things on her own, but I wanted to remind her that she wasn't facing any of this by herself. I'd promised to never leave her side and that was a promise I fully intended to keep.

"Let's get this over with." Levi walked right up to the front door. I hung back a few steps behind him. I figured he was more than capable of handling the brunt of her annoyance himself. He was the king after all.

He knocked on the door.

A few moments later the door was opened by a servant. "Good evening, your highness."

"Is my grandmother still up?"

"I believe she is." The servant stepped back to allow Levi to enter.

He put out his arm to stop Daisy and I from following.

Levi pushed his arm out of the way. "They are with me."

The servant nodded and bowed awkwardly, and I led Daisy inside the large entryway.

Daisy gazed around her in wonder. This was her second visit to a Laurent house that evening, and she had probably already connected the dots and realized they had certain things in common. Both homes had modern ornate designs that spared no expense. Her eyes went directly to the crystal chandelier hanging above us.

Levi looked at me. "Why don't you wait here?"

"You sure?"

"Yes. I need to make sure Georgina is ready to see

visitors."

"Of course I am ready to receive visitors." Georgina walked down the sweeping staircase. "Allison told me to expect you and some guests." She walked down and right over to Levi. "Lovely to see you, Leviathan, but I hope there is a good reason for such a late visit. Allison assured me I'd understand once you explained."

"Hi grandma." He hugged her.

Daisy smiled. I'm sure it was interesting to watch the king greet his grandmother. I wondered if it made him seem more human and less royal.

"Owen, how nice to see you." She kissed me formally on the cheek. She'd always liked me, but I didn't really understand why. I wasn't exactly from a high ranking family.

"Do you mean that?" Levi asked. I never would have had the nerve.

"Possibly." She turned to Daisy and gave her a long look. "And this must be Daisy. Allison said I would like you."

Daisy flushed and did this half bow thing.

Levi chuckled, but Georgina merely held out a hand. "I'm Georgina Laurent. Pleasure to meet you."

"Pleasure to meet you too." Daisy kept eye contact with her. That in itself was impressive for a first meeting.

"Allison told me you needed information on ancient beings and lands." She looked between Daisy and me.

"Yes." I was glad we didn't have to go through the whole story again.

"Boys, why don't you start reading through the books I laid out in the library?" She gestured down the hall. "Daisy and I are going to have a talk." She turned and walked out of the room leaving us no room to argue.

"I guess that means I follow." Daisy shrugged.

"You'll be fine. I can already tell she likes you." Levi smiled reassuringly.

"I can probably thank your wife for that." She hurried after Georgina into the hall.

"You look more nervous than she does." Levi ribbed.

"I'm allowed to worry about her."

"You are, but you also have to accept she can take care of herself."

"Quit trying to sound all wise because you're married now."

"I've always been wise. I just understand women more now." He laughed and headed down the hallway.

The doors to the library were ajar, and we walked right in. The last time I'd been inside, I'd been a kid. I remembered Levi's grandfather reading us a story about ancient dragons, and our friend Jared declaring he was going to own one someday. At the time we'd laughed. Dragons were long extinct, but if Allures were here, then what else could be?

"Should we divide and conquer?" Levi handed me two books.

"Sure." I accepted the books and took a seat in an upholstered armchair.

Levi sat down on the chair next to mine with his books. "I guess we should look for any mention of Energo."

"I don't see any other choice."

"We're going to figure this out. Georgina knows nearly everything. If anyone knows, it's her."

"Then why is she having us read these books?"

"Because she wanted time alone with Daisy."

"Then why bother reading them?"

"Because you love this girl." He didn't need to say anything else.

I opened the first heavy, dusty volume and started scanning the pages. "Think these will ever be available electronically?"

Levi laughed. "Not as long as Georgina is the one in charge of them."

"It's probably more secure this way, but it's dangerous to have only one copy."

"I'm sure Georgina has some sort of backup."

"Good point." I continued scanning through the pages. Other than the word Energo I wasn't certain what I was looking for, but I figured any mention of secret cities or places would help.

Levi set aside one of his books. "We knew the Allures weren't dead. We shouldn't be so surprised."

"All I ever heard was they 'left.'" I'd never been curious enough to ask more questions. I was regretting that attitude now.

"But they had to have left to go somewhere."

"And you think that place is Energo?" It was the only lead we had, so I hoped he agreed.

"I'm guessing there has to be some connection."

"That's what I'm banking on."

We spent another twenty minutes searching through books. If we could only find Energo, maybe we'd find answers.

five

daisy

"You don't have to look so petrified." Georgina sat perfectly straight in her chair. I'd already relayed my story to her. I figured holding back any information would only hurt me.

"You can be intimidating." I wasn't generally scared of old ladies, but Georgina had this air about her that made it difficult to speak coherently or make eye contact.

"You say that as though it is a bad thing."

"Not bad, but it explains my nerves."

"Straighten up your shoulders," she scolded.

I straightened in my chair. "With everything else going on, I haven't been worried about my posture."

"What does having a lot going on have to do with sitting correctly?"

"I'm just saying—"

"Don't just say anything. Everything spoken should be for a reason. Once we get this little problem fixed, I want you to start meeting with me for lessons. If you are going to be

41

mating with the king's chief advisor, you must look and act the part."

"Mating… uh?"

"Don't play games, Daisy. I rather like your honest and upfront personality. Owen would have never brought you here if he didn't plan to spend his life with you, and from what you've told me, one of your greatest fears with becoming an Allure is losing your feelings for him. Therefore, you will be his mate."

I wondered if she realized Owen had taken a break from his job at The Society.

She read my mind. "Owen will return to serve Levi. He has always been dedicated to The Society, and no amount of soul searching will change that. And neither will you. In fact your presence in his life will make him more dedicated to the cause. He will have the motivation and focus he needs. The woman plays a very important role in the man's career."

"That sounds sexist." My lack of a filter was going to get me in trouble.

"But it's not sexist, is it? I am simply saying that in a relationship each partner advances the other. I have no doubt that he will help you achieve your goals, whatever they are."

"That's not how all relationships work." I'd witnessed plenty that were nothing like that.

"If a relationship doesn't work that way, it is useless. Rubbish. Appearance and tradition are important, but more important is that each member of a couple feel supported and important. Mark my words, Daisy. One day you will understand."

"Hopefully. I mean if we can't stop this change I probably won't understand because I'll never have a real relationship."

"Do you truly doubt you'll be successful? Even after watching Owen's optimism and determination?"

"There's only so far that can go."

"It won't be easy. It's going to be difficult, and like all truly important journeys in life it is equally likely to kill you as save you, but in the end you will have given it your all."

"You talk about death as though it's nothing." Death was the ultimate end. It had such finality that it couldn't be shrugged off.

"Is losing your humanity, your propensity to feel, not worse than death? What do we have if not our emotions? They are what guide us."

"I don't want to die." I could hear the fear in my voice. Death terrified me, but would it be worse than becoming an Allure? Neither sounded appealing.

"Of course not." She crossed her legs. "And the hope is you don't. I am merely reminding you that there are things worse than death."

"I'm hoping in all of this you have a plan."

"Of course I do. I always have a plan."

"And what is this plan?"

"First, we all get some rest. Then first thing in the morning we pay a visit to our friend Mayanne."

"You know her?"

"Of course. Didn't Owen tell you? She is one of my oldest friends. She lives near here."

So that's where we'd been. I'd never figured out exactly where the house was. I'd been more concerned with losing blood, and Owen. "But she wasn't able to get rid of the paste's effect last time."

"Because she didn't quite know what it was. I will speak

with her so she has time to prepare."

"What about the guys? What if they found something?"

"They aren't going to find anything."

"Then why did you tell them to read?"

"Because we needed time to talk."

I laughed. "Do you do things like that a lot?"

"Often. I am sure Levi figured it out quickly."

"Should we go find them?"

"You go do that. I will see to the preparation of the guest rooms."

"I don't want to put you out." Not that there was really a choice other than sleeping in the car. It would be pointless to drive back and forth another time.

"It's no trouble." She stood up. "Levi will know where to go. Sleep well, and I will see you all in the morning." She walked out of the room.

"Oh, thanks." I belatedly responded after she left the room. She definitely knew how to make an exit.

I wandered around the first floor until I found the library. Both Owen and Levi looked up as soon as I reached the door.

"Learn anything?" Owen asked.

"We're going to see Mayanne tomorrow."

"She thinks there is more she can do?"

I shrugged. "Evidently. She knows more too, but I get the sense she's only going to reveal things one step at a time."

"Some sleep would be good for you." He smiled.

"Aren't you going to sleep?"

"I might try."

"My bet is she'll put you in separate rooms, but I also know she won't mind if Owen visits. Just be on good behavior." Levi grinned.

"Of course." I put a hand to my chest. "I'm not crazy. I respect the rules of someone's home."

"You are very concerned with being polite." Levi shifted his weight from foot to foot.

"It's how I was raised."

"Allie is too, but in a different way. Less southern."

"Are you going to go home?" I felt bad about him leaving his wife alone for so long.

"Yeah. I'll fly home and be back in the morning. I am sure Owen can take care of anything you need."

Owen shook his head. "Go already."

"You know where the rooms are?" Levi asked.

"Upstairs and to the left."

"Great. Good night you two." He strolled off toward the front door.

"Ready?" Owen asked.

"Not quite yet." I walked further into the library.

"You are a very curious person."

I turned back to look at him. "You think? I spent years searching for you."

"Was it for me, or what I represented?"

"Oh no. None of that. I had enough psycho-analysis from Georgia."

"Oh? In what way?"

"Just about there being things worse than death, but I was searching for you because I wanted to find you. Not because of well, what you are."

"But would I have intrigued you as much without the wings?"

"Why are you doing this? Aren't you supposed to be reassuring me?"

"Humor me."

"I wanted you before I saw your wings. Before you saved me. Call it love at first sight or whatever, but one glance was all it took." I remembered the first moment I saw him in the bar. He'd blown me off afterward, but it didn't matter. I still couldn't get him out of my head.

"Yeah, you're still there." He grinned.

"What?"

"I wanted to see if your emotional memory was affected. Clearly it's not. You don't doubt your feelings for me."

"It's the only feeling I truly know is real."

"Because it is." His arms moved around me from behind, and he pulled me back into his chest. "I'm sorry this is how things turned out. I never should have walked away from you that night. I should have stayed. I thought I was doing you a favor by staying out of your life."

"None of this is your fault."

"If I'd searched harder or asked Levi for help finding you, we could have fixed things earlier."

"But maybe that wouldn't have made a difference. We'll never know."

"I want you to get some sleep." He nodded toward the doorway.

"Abrupt change of conversation."

"I know you're wide awake, but you need sleep. Who knows what tomorrow is going to involve?"

"Will you stay with me?" I didn't want to be alone. I'd never get sleep that way, and I wanted Owen as close as possible.

"Yes. Levi said it himself. Georgina won't care."

"Good." I took his hand. "Then let's sleep."

We walked up the sweeping stairway, and Owen led us to one of the bedrooms.

"Are you even going to pretend to sleep in another?"

"Nope. I don't want to let you out of my sight."

"You did twice tonight."

"Technically yes," he admitted, "But only when I had to."

"Do you think it's okay if I showered?"

"Of course. There's a bathroom through there." He pointed to a door.

"Thanks. I need it." I kissed him gently on the lips before stepping into the bathroom and closing the door.

He knocked seconds later. "Hey Daisy, Georgina left this out for you."

I opened the door and found Owen holding a night shirt.

"Great, I was thinking I'd love to sleep in something else."

"I'd love for you to sleep in nothing, but that's not an option."

"Nope, not in this house." I accepted the nightshirt. "Be right out."

"Take your time." He gently closed the door.

I stripped off my clothes and turned on the shower. I felt dirty and exhausted, and if the shower could take care of the first, the bed would be ready for the second. I stepped underneath the warm stream, trying to wash away the grit and grime of the past few days. It felt like so much had changed so quickly, but more than anything I had knowledge. I knew what was happening to me, and as helpful as that was, it also terrified me and made things tons harder to handle.

I could have stayed under the warm water forever, but that meant staying away from Owen. I craved him like I craved nothing else in life. Staying away from him would be like a moth avoiding a flame. Impossible.

I got out and dried off, eagerly slipping into the old fashioned nightgown. I couldn't have cared what it looked like, even if Owen was going to see it. It was clean and soft, and those were two very important characteristics to me at the moment.

I opened the door to find Owen lying on the bed in pajama pants and a t-shirt. "Did you get pajamas too?"

"Yes." He smiled. "And the funny thing is, Georgina left them in the same room with yours."

I laughed. "I don't know why she would have assumed we'd wind up in the same room."

"Me either." He slipped under the covers and held open one side. "Going to join me?"

I ran a hand through my wet hair. "If you don't mind getting wet."

He waggled an eyebrow. "With you, never."

"Clean thoughts tonight."

"The cleanest. We're talking about water. You can't get cleaner than that."

I slipped in beside him. "I'm exhausted."

"You're finally admitting it?"

I nodded before snuggling in to his side. "I can barely keep my eyes open."

"The beauty is you don't have to keep them open. In fact you need to keep them closed."

"Maybe Mayanne will be able to do more this time."

"Maybe." He ran a hand down my back. "And you said it yourself, Georgina knows more. She's making us wait because we need to. She could see how tired you were before you even could."

"She's perceptive but also calculating."

"She has our interests at heart. Don't doubt that." He traced small circles down my back. The touch felt great even through the silky material of the nightgown.

"I need you to promise me something." Georgina's words about the danger in all journeys ran through my head.

"What?' He stopped the motion of his fingers.

"If saving me means risking yourself, you'll walk away."

"Absolutely not." He took my face in his hands. "That's ridiculous."

"But you are healthy. You have nothing to fear. Why should you walk into danger for me?"

"Because I love you." His eyes pleaded with me to believe him. I knew he was being honest, but was that enough?

"But is love worth sacrificing your life?"

"Yes." He kissed me hard on the lips. I didn't respond at first, ready to follow-up with all my arguments for why his life was more important, but he drowned them out by pushing for access to my mouth. I greedily sucked in everything he was willing to give, letting his taste and touch overwhelm my senses until I couldn't concentrate on anything else. The kiss seemed to suspend time, and it felt as though we'd lost ourselves in each other's arms. Neither of us pushed for anything else. It wasn't the time or place, and we didn't need more. The kiss expressed everything we wanted to share.

Finally, we broke the kiss and lay in each other's arms.

"Did that clear up all of your questions and concerns?" he whispered against my neck.

"Yes. I don't want you putting yourself in danger, but nothing I can say is going to change your mind."

"I'm a Pteron. I'm strong, and we have each other. I'm not going to get hurt, and neither are you."

"You're too good to be true."

"Not any more than you." He pulled me up on top of him. "You are so much better than all of my dreams and memories. I don't know if it's because you've gotten even better, or if my imagination and memory are lacking."

"I'll go with the first."

"I thought you'd say that." He wrapped his arms around me.

"You know I can't actually sleep this way."

"Why not?" He moved underneath me. "Are you trying to say I'm not comfortable to lay on?"

"Not if I'm trying to keep my thoughts and actions clean."

He laughed. "Good point." He gently rolled me off him to the side.

I rested my head on his chest. "This is perfect."

"I'm never going to be able to sleep alone again."

"You barely need to sleep."

"Even so."

"You're not the only one." I draped my arm over his body. "I've never felt as safe and comfortable as when I'm with you."

"It's a good thing we're going to be spending all our nights together then, huh?"

"I guess so." I smiled.

"Try to get some sleep."

"I will. You'll stay here?"

"I thought the kiss got everything across. I'm not leaving you."

"Good," I replied sleepily. I let my heavy eyes close, and I yawned.

He went back to rubbing my back. "Sleep well, my love."

"You too," I mumbled as I drifted off into sleep.

six

owen

"Owen, what's the matter?" Daisy's voice was higher pitched than usual. She stood at the foot of the bed wearing only a t-shirt.

"Nothing." I sat up in bed and rubbed my eyes. "You sound different."

"No, I don't. You're imagining things again." She crawled up my body slowly before straddling me on top of the sheets.

"Are you sick?" I studied her eyes. They were glazed over, as though she were high or something.

"No." She shook her head. "Stop worrying."

"I can't." I closed my eyes.

"Yes, you can." She brushed her lips against mine. "You can stop feeling anytime you want."

I opened my eyes. "Daisy? Is that even you anymore?"

She laughed a laugh that wasn't hers. "What do you think? Aren't you the expert on me?"

I woke up with a start, glad to see the first signs of

sunlight through the sheer window shades. I ran my hands down Daisy's back while she slept peacefully. She was still Daisy. We'd find a way to stop the change. I refused to believe the dreams were anything prophetic. They were only manifestations of my fears. They'd eventually go away once we got rid of the Allure in her once and for all.

She stirred beside me.

"Good morning." I wanted her to wake up. I needed to hear her voice and see her eyes. I knew the dream wasn't real, but it was difficult to shake.

"Hey." She opened her perfectly normal and beautiful hazel eyes slowly.

"Sleep okay?"

"Yes. You?"

"All right." I didn't like lying to her.

"What's wrong?" She sat up.

I pulled her into my arms. "A nightmare. Nothing to worry about."

"What kind of nightmare?" Her brow furrowed.

"Nothing worth repeating."

She sighed. "We need to find Energo. We have no time to waste."

"I know."

A loud knock on the door had us both jumping.

"It's me," Levi called. "Allie sent some clothes for Daisy. I'll leave them out here. Georgina is already up and about." Allie was good at making sure people had what they needed. She'd made a great impression on Daisy, and I hoped they'd have a chance to get to know each other under better circumstances soon enough.

I waited until I heard his footsteps disappear before

opening the door. I retrieved the bundle of clothes and set them down on the bed.

Daisy looked through them while I hastily got dressed.

She picked up a dress. "Why don't you head on down? I'll meet you down there."

I assumed she wanted privacy, so I didn't argue. I kissed her gently on the lips before heading downstairs to wait for her.

I paced the room while I waited for Daisy to get ready. I didn't want to rush her, but I was anxious to get moving.

"Leviathan, will you be coming with us?" Georgina floated into the room in the way only she could.

"As long as I'm invited."

She swatted at his arm. "As if the king needs an invitation."

"To impose on you does require one."

"I want you to come. My feeling is these two will be leaving for a new destination once we are done at Mayanne's. I will need you to escort me home."

"Of course," Levi replied quickly. I tried not to dwell on it, but what kind of destination would Energo be? Why wasn't it on any of the maps?

"Sorry!" Daisy hurried down the stairs wearing a knee length blue dress.

"Do not apologize. A lady never should when she takes the proper time to get ready, and you look lovely." Georgina shot Daisy an uncharacteristically bright smile. "Allison's clothes fit you nicely."

"I'm sure this dress is a little bit shorter on her, but it works."

"I went through the clothes before Levi delivered them, and I noticed she gave you several options. I am glad you chose the dress rather than the slacks for today, but you may need the pants where you go next."

"Does that mean you know where we're going?" Daisy asked hopefully.

"Not necessarily, but I do understand a dress isn't suitable for all occasions."

"You look beautiful." I took in how she looked in the form fitting dress. It was the type of dress Allie wore a lot, and by how comfortable Daisy looked in it, it was probably her style too.

"Thank you." She beamed and walked over. "It's definitely nice to be in clean clothes."

"I will make sure you have everything you need for your trip, but let's see Mayanne first."

I wanted to question Georgina about the trip, but I kept my mouth closed. She'd tell us when she was ready, and rushing her would only get us on her bad side. We couldn't afford that.

"Did you sleep well?" Georgina asked.

"Yes." Daisy smiled. "Thank you for the hospitality."

"My pleasure. You are a guest in my home. I hope next time you are visiting under different circumstances." Georgina seemed to be trying to bite back a smile. She wasn't the type to smile so much. Maybe she'd mellowed out now that Levi was king, and he and Allie had had an heir.

"Leviathan, if you don't mind, I would prefer you drove. I don't want to trouble my driver." Georgina would have never been concerned about troubling an employee. That was her excuse for not wanting the driver to see where we were going.

"Absolutely." Levi took his grandmother's arm. "You

know how much I hate letting someone else drive me around."

"It's your mother's fault. She didn't properly expose you to genuine royal life."

Levi let out a heavy sigh. "Could we please avoid any criticism of my mom today? I thought you two were finally getting along."

"We are." Georgina adjusted the strap of her purse on her arm. "But that doesn't mean I won't point out her inadequacies."

Daisy gasped. Georgina turned to her. "Do you disagree?"

"No. Sorry." Daisy looked away.

"Very well, let's go." Georgina headed for the front door. Once out on the porch she handed me the key to lock the door. I did it without complaint. I wasn't surprised by any of Georgina's idiosyncrasies any more. I handed back the key.

Daisy and I settled into the back seat of the car, as Levi pulled back out onto the long country road.

"Did you talk to Mayanne?" Daisy asked as soon as the house was out of view. It was as though she waited until it would be difficult for us to cancel the visit.

"Yes, and she's expecting us."

"Does she know anything about Energo?" Daisy asked. "Did she have any solutions to my problem?"

Georgina didn't turn around. "She knows something about it, and she thinks she can delay the change."

"Really?" Daisy asked excitedly. "That's awesome."

"She can't stop things completely, but it appears that your biggest obstacle right now is time. If we can get you more of that, you will have a far better chance of success."

"Absolutely." Daisy's entire body relaxed. She wore a real

smile on her face for the rest of the trip. I hoped Georgina hadn't gotten her hopes up for nothing. How disappointed would she be if it turned out Mayanne couldn't help? I kept my concerns to myself, or I tried to.

"Stop." Daisy put a hand on my leg.

"Stop what?"

"Getting discouraged. I can feel it, which makes me angry, and that's not a good thing."

"I'm sorry." I quickly apologized.

"I'm going to bundle myself back up in the happy, relieved thoughts."

"Focusing on the good doesn't get rid of the bad." Levi kept glancing at her in the rearview mirror.

"Let her have her comfort." Georgina patted Levi's arm. "She deserves it."

"You don't have the urge to manipulate, do you?" He asked suspiciously.

"You think I want to mess with people?" Daisy laughed dryly. "You think I want to hurt them?"

I touched her leg gently. "It's okay. Ignore him."

"Ignore me? Ignore the king?" Levi slowed the car. "If she can't handle me asking questions without getting upset, she's bound to go off if you guys hit any real trouble."

Daisy sighed. "You think I don't know? I wish I could stay calm."

"Try harder." Levi's hands tightened on the wheel.

"She's trying as hard as she can." I ran my thumb over her hand.

"I hate what's happening to me. I have no control." Daisy grazed her lip with her teeth.

"We know." Georgina turned around. "But hating

something doesn't make it go away."

"Don't I know?"

"Leviathan will hold his tongue until we get to Mayanne's." There was a warning in her tone.

Daisy closed her eyes. I unbuckled my seatbelt so I could move closer to her. As much as I liked to pretend I was doing it for her benefit, I was also doing it for my own. I wanted to be near her. I needed to know she was real and right there next to me.

"Turn right up ahead, Leviathan." Georgina pointed at the windshield.

"Has Mayanne moved?"

"No, but we need to stop for breakfast."

"Stop for breakfast?" Levi asked. "You can't be serious."

"Of course I can be, and I am. We can't start a busy day without a good breakfast."

"But we're running out of time." Daisy spoke softly, as though she were worried about upsetting Georgina.

"A good breakfast is worth the time. You can't face today without it."

Levi turned right as directed.

"What if you dropped me off at Mayanne's and then had breakfast?" Daisy sounded desperate.

"Nonsense. You need the nourishment more than any of us." Georgina shifted in her seat. "There is a lovely diner right up this street. You will see it on the left."

"A diner? You eat at a diner?" Levi laughed dryly.

"Is there anything wrong with that?" Georgina turned to look at him.

"Not specifically, but it's surprising." Levi was one of the few people brave or stupid enough to talk to Georgina that way.

"The food here is up to my standards."

"If you say so." Levi pulled into the gravel lot of a diner that seemed to be called exactly that. Diner. The lot was packed full of cars and trucks. That didn't bode well for quick service.

"It's going to be okay," I reassured Daisy. She hadn't said anything since asking to be dropped off, and I knew that wasn't a good thing.

She waited until we were out of the car to reply. Levi and Georgina went on ahead and disappeared inside the building. "How is eating breakfast going to help anything? The thought of food makes my stomach churn. I need to see Mayanne. We have to find out what the heck Energo is."

"I know." I was tempted to fly off with her myself, but Georgina usually had her reasons. If she was insisting we stop for breakfast, she probably had a purpose. Besides, it was broad daylight. Flying would be risky. "Let's eat something to make her happy. After that we can leave ourselves if we have to."

She kissed my cheek. "Thank you."

I pulled her close and kissed her lightly on the lips. "I'm here with you. Don't forget that."

"I won't." She gripped my arm.

We walked into the diner where Levi and Georgina had already disappeared. I glanced around. There wasn't an empty table in the place.

"Great," Daisy mumbled. I didn't bother replying. She had every right to be annoyed.

"Excuse me miss, may I help you with anything?" A grinning waiter walked over. It was the bellboy all over again.

"We're waiting for a table."

"For two?" He ignored me, and let his eyes rake over her. If I hadn't known about the magical rationale for his response, the guy would have been in trouble.

"For four." Daisy glanced around. "We have two more with us."

"I can serve you at the bar if you're hungry. You don't have to wait." He licked his lips.

Magic or not, I was ready to pounce.

"I'm sure you could serve all of us." Daisy smiled back. "Wouldn't you like that? To make me happy?"

"Uh sure. Of course. I would love to make you happy. There is room at the bar for four." The guy gestured to the completely full bar. His vacant expression and glassy eyes said it all.

I touched Daisy's arm. "You don't want to do this."

She shook me off. "Thank you. We'd prefer a table. I'm sure you'd like to find one for me? A booth maybe? It would make me really happy."

"I'll take care of that right away." He walked away.

I took both of Daisy's hands in mine and looked into her eyes. "Daisy, stop."

She said nothing at first, but then she blinked as a look of horror and fear spread across her face. "Oh my god. I manipulated." She leaned forward and hugged her knees. "Where's Georgina? We have to go. I can't handle this." She blinked back a few tears.

I helped her up to standing. "You're crying, and that's a good thing. You're feeling guilty."

"I manipulated that guy."

"Not on purpose." I glanced around. Where the hell were

Levi and Georgina?

"Your table is ready." The waiter returned with a huge smile. "It's a booth by the window." A family rushed toward the entrance angrily.

"Did you kick those people out?" She asked, horrified.

"Yes." The waiter appeared confused. "I did."

"Daisy, Owen!" Georgina called from a table tucked to the side of the bar. "We're over here."

"I'm so sorry," she whispered to the waiter before hurrying over to where Georgina and Levi sat with an older couple.

"What took you so long?" Levi pulled two chairs over to the small table.

"We were talking," I answered quickly. Telling Levi about the manipulation wouldn't be smart. I wanted his help, which made it worth keeping him in the dark.

"Daisy, how nice to meet you." The older woman seated across from Georgina smiled. "Very pretty name."

"Thank you."

"Are you all ready to order?" The same waiter approached us.

Daisy looked down at the table. I waited as everyone else ordered before taking a guess and ordering her what I was ordering myself—pancakes.

She nodded, but still refused to look up.

The waiter stared at her way longer than necessary.

"Is there something else you need?" I tried to subtly get him to walk away.

"Do you want anything else?" He looked at her, as though that would make her turn. He still looked confused, although his eyes had returned to normal.

She shook her head. "No thanks."

He ducked down and peered around to see her face. "Are you sure?"

"She said no." Levi turned his finger around in a circle by his face. He was wrong, the guy wasn't crazy. He was enchanted.

"Please put in our orders." Daisy finally looked up. "Thank you."

The waiter nodded and hurried away.

The other woman at the table smiled. "I haven't seen that in years."

"Seen what?" I asked.

"A woman affect a man that way. I had an old friend. A lovely girl. She had a flower name too. Violet." She rubbed her forehead. "I always wondered what happened to her."

Daisy and I exchanged looks. There was no way this was a coincidence.

Georgina smiled. "My friend Myrtle here worked with me when I was queen. She often stood in for me at affairs when I couldn't make it."

Myrtle laughed. "She means she took pity on me and let me have some excitement in my life. It's how I met Bob." She touched the arm of the man next to her.

"That's great." I looked at Georgina. What was the end game? What did Myrtle know?

"Is Violet the same girl you told me about? The one who disappeared into thin air one night?"

"Yes. She's the one." Myrtle's face fell.

Bob patted her back. "It's all right, Myrtle. You tried everything you could to help her."

"Help her with what?" Daisy asked.

"She was looking for a man. It's why I invited her to the Applerose Gala. I'd found him and knew he was coming."

"Did they meet? She and that man?"

Myrtle shook her head. "No. That was what I'll never understand. Violet spent the night watching him but never approached." Myrtle turned to us. "And if you knew Violet you'd understand she wasn't shy. There was something else holding her back. She seemed so sad and vulnerable in a way I'd never seen her look before. Usually she was the happiest girl in the room."

"What happened next?" Daisy pressed.

"She was there one moment and gone the next. She never said goodbye, and when I went by to see her at her home, she had left. Vanished really. We filed a police report, but that was that."

"I remember the disappearance. They must have interrogated half-a-dozen men afterward." Georgina seemed lost in thought.

The table fell into an uncomfortable silence. What was the significance of this story? Georgina must have known Violet was an Allure.

Before I could ask any questions, our food was brought to the table. Daisy only picked at her plate, and I knew it had nothing to do with what I'd ordered.

seven

owen

Levi turned down another side road, and I knew we were getting close. I braced myself. I hoped Mayanne would know how to stall the effects, but there was a chance she couldn't. Was there also a chance she could make it worse?

I couldn't think that way. We needed all the help we could get, and so far Mayanne was our best bet.

Levi turned off onto a dirt road, and I knew we were almost there. Mayanne lived miles from anyone else. I wasn't sure how much of it came from her being a witch, and how much came from her personality.

We turned up the dirt drive, and I kissed Daisy on the forehead. "You ready for this?"

"As ready as I'm going to be." She'd been quiet since breakfast. I knew that she was probably beating herself up about manipulating the waiter. I understood why it upset her. It freaked me out too.

"Either Mayanne got a new car, or she has company."

Georgina pointed to an SUV parked by the front door of the rambling home.

"Stay here." Levi parked.

"I'll come with you."

"No. Stay with them." Levi's eyes gave me all the warning I needed. I knew he was right. One of us needed to stay with Georgina and Daisy. They were human after all.

Before Levi could make it a few steps the front door opened, and Mayanne stepped out.

I got right out of the car, and Daisy followed. I opened Georgina's door and helped her out.

"I need you to all stay calm." Mayanne walked out onto the rickety front porch.

"Stay calm?" I looked at the tall and willowy woman. "Why would you tell us that?"

"Who's visiting you, Mayanne?" Georgina walked over to her friend.

"They aren't here for me, but stay calm. They may be of help."

I didn't need to hear the names to know who the visitors were. "Are they inside?"

Mayanne nodded. "Stay calm, Owen."

"I'll try."

Daisy slipped her hand into mine. "Stay calm for my sake."

"I'll try," I repeated my words.

Mayanne, Georgina, and Levi walked in first, and Levi held open the door for us to walk inside.

"Hello, old friends." Hugh smirked.

Any thoughts of staying calm disappeared. "What the hell are you doing here?" I didn't think about the company I was in, I said exactly what was on my mind.

"We're here for the same reason you are. We want to help Daisy." Violet smiled.

"Help her? You mean take away any chance she has to stay human?"

"If we wanted that we'd have left you guys to your own devices, but we do care." Violet caught my eye.

"Where's Roland?" Daisy spoke for the first time since walking in.

"He's not here." Hugh shrugged. "We thought it best if he stayed away."

"Why?"

"Because his interests are too complicated."

"His interests?" Levi asked. He stepped toward the Allures. "What kind of interests does he have beyond the ones you do?"

"She has his maker's essence. He is drawn to her, and he doesn't mind the new packaging." Hugh smirked.

I was in his face in a blur. "The packaging? Don't you ever talk about Daisy that way."

"I thought you'd prefer it to me saying he's attracted to her."

"Shut up!" Daisy wrung her hands. "Shut up all of you."

Georgina cleared her throat.

"Sorry." Daisy looked at her. "But I'm not going to stand here and listen to this. You say you want to help me? Then help me. Mayanne thinks she can buy me time. Let's see what she can do."

Mayanne nodded. "I can't do anything with a crowd."

"That's fine. Daisy and I will go with you. Everyone else can wait." That was the only logical solution.

"Not a chance." Violet shook her head. "We have a vested interest in this too."

"Because of the essence and not Daisy. She's the important part."

"They are both important." Violet pressed her lips into a firm line.

"Daisy is more important. I don't care what you say, that's the truth." I stood my ground.

"I'll go with Mayanne by myself. Everyone else can stay out here." Daisy avoided my eyes when she spoke.

"You don't have to do that. I promised I'd stay with you."

"And I can't handle more of this arguing. I am nervous and freaking out already. I don't need anyone making it worse."

"She'll be fine, Owen. We'll only be upstairs." Mayanne touched my arm reassuringly. "You know I'd never hurt her."

"I know…"

Georgina repeated Mayanne's words. "She will be fine."

Before Levi could join in and agree with the two women, I cut him off. "I know she will be fine, but that doesn't mean I want to leave her."

"It's not leaving me if I'm asking you to wait here." Daisy's face softened. "And I expect you to be waiting when we're done."

"Of course." I smiled. She was the one going through the most physically. I owed it to her to hold myself together. I needed to be strong. "I'll be right here."

"Come on, hun." Mayanne put a hand on Daisy's back and led her toward the doorway.

I had to fight the urge to follow. As soon as they disappeared I turned back to Violet. "What is really going on?"

"We already told you. We're here to help." Violet rolled her eyes.

"But why?" I pressed. "Why are you helping?"

"Because I like Daisy."

"But you can't even feel. You can't actually care."

"I'm not heartless." Violet sighed. "I may not be able to feel true emotion, but that doesn't mean I can't feel others'. There's an intensity in Daisy." She looked off.

"Her love for Owen is strong." Georgina smiled warmly. "It's strong enough that it got your attention."

"It's what's keeping her fighting the change, isn't it?" Violet turned to Georgina. "Otherwise she'd have given in."

Georgina nodded. "I'm sure there is more at work. She loves her family I have no doubt, but her feelings for Owen are intense, maybe part of that originated from the way they met or the magic she was exposed to, but it doesn't matter now. Her heart is what it is."

"That kind of love is rare." Hugh rocked back on his heels. "It's hard not to play with it."

Violet glared at him. "You will not make things any harder than they already are for her. No one will."

Hugh scrunched up his face. "It's almost pathetic."

My hands balled into fists. "Shut up."

"You're lucky we left Roland behind." Hugh grinned. "You'd be even more annoyed at him."

"Where is he?" I had to ask.

"I guess leaving him behind is making it sound nicer than it was." Hugh stuffed his hands in his pockets.

"Meaning?" Levi asked. He'd been unusually quiet.

"Meaning we had to use force. He's drawn to her, but we

couldn't have him getting in the way."

"You used force against your own?" Levi seemed surprised. Very little surprised him.

"As if you should talk? You have imprisoned Pterons before."

"Not my friends."

"Maybe not your social friends, but friends of The Society."

"You have him imprisoned?" I asked. "That seems extreme even for you."

"Not imprisoned so much as distracted."

"What does that mean?" Levi stepped toward them.

"Why so curious?" Violet asked. "Looking for new ways to control your people?"

"No."

"Oh." Violet crossed her arms. "Got it. You want to know how to subdue an Allure. Now that we're back, you're worried."

"We're not worried." He straightened out. Violet had him ruffled.

"You are. You don't know what to do now that older, stronger creatures are in your midst."

"He is not worried." Georgina stepped between her grandson and the Allures. "The King of The Society does not fear others. He is only doing his job. Protecting his people."

"I like you." Violet studied Georgina. "Why aren't you in charge?"

"Because she's human," Hugh said matter-of-factly. "A human would never be put in charge of the Society."

"Our mates still play a major role in our decision making. That has been the case since the Laurents have been in power." Georgina held her chin up.

Violet seemed pensive. "I like you better than your predecessors."

"My dad?" Levi asked.

"No, the family before."

"You were really around for that?" Georgina seemed to be looking at Violet with new eyes.

"Yes. We live long lives." Violet's face fell into a wistful expression. "There are good parts and bad parts about that gift."

I thought about what Myrtle had said. How Violet had searched for the guy and then disappeared. How did that all tie in? I sensed there was a significance we needed to understand.

"But you call it a gift, so that already speaks for a lot." Georgina walked toward a sitting room and set down her purse. The rest of us followed.

"It is a gift, but even the best gifts come with strings."

"You were in love." Georgina reached out and touched Violet's hand. "That's why you understand Daisy." Georgina turned to me. "Absent of true feeling or not, this one still has a heart."

"Then Daisy might too. Even if we fail…" Levi started.

Violet shook her head. "It's not the same. She won't be able to give him what he needs, and he what she needs. It would never be love. And it would take her years to even remember why she cared so much."

Georgina took Violet's hands in hers. "I'm sure he was a good man."

Levi and I exchanged looks. Georgina had softened over the past few years, but this was extreme for her. This had to tie into Myrtle's story.

"I barely remember why I loved him, but I know I did."

"How old are you?" Levi asked.

"Leviathan Laurent." Georgina scowled. "You were raised better than to ever ask a woman her age."

"I don't think that rule applies for an Allure."

"I'm old. Older than anyone you've ever met."

"Older than me." Hugh laughed.

"Age stops having meaning after a while." She turned to me. "Everything does."

"Mayanne is going to find a way to delay the change."

"She will. We discussed it before you arrived." Violet spoke calmly.

"What? What did you discuss?" I needed to know everything.

Violet sighed. "Calm down. If you want to help Daisy, you are going to have to learn to trust me."

"How can I trust someone who doesn't feel?"

"Don't let Daisy hear that," Hugh took a seat on a couch. "She's already starting to change. My guess is that would insult her."

"Everything will insult her right now." I slumped down in a chair. "I don't know what to do. I just wish I could make it all go away."

"There will be nothing 'just' about it. Even if Mayanne is successful in delaying the change, it's still going to be a difficult journey."

"Journey? What is with all this journey talk?" I needed to know more.

"You don't know yet?" Violet turned to Georgina. "You feel confident, determined. I assumed that meant you knew."

"I know the place isn't of this world." Georgina took a seat on a chair across from me.

"No. It's not."

"Where is Energo?" Levi asked. "Be frank with me."

"Your matriarch is correct. It's of another world, but it's not Energo you need to find."

"Then what is?" I was tired of the games, the never ending circles.

"It's Mount Majest. The palace at the top of the highest mountain in all of the worlds. You can only get there through Energo though."

"I take it you know where to go?" Levi asked.

"Absolutely."

"Tell us." I didn't bother with being polite. They'd worn out any politeness I had in me.

"No." She shook her head.

"Tell us." I repeated.

She shook her head. "No. I will show you though."

"No. You are not coming." I didn't trust the Allures. They had too many of their own motives, and we knew almost nothing about them.

"The creatures you need to talk to will not give you an audience."

"Then what's the point of going?"

"They will however give me one."

"Who are these creatures anyway?"

"The Elders." Violet tossed her dark hair off her shoulder.

"They are as close to the gods as…" Georgina trailed off.

"They do say we descend from the gods don't they?" Violet gazed off into the distance.

"And you think they will help?"

71

"No. I doubt they will."

I froze. "Then I ask again, why bother seeing them?"

"Because they are your only hope."

eight

daisy

Mayanne led me into the same room I'd slept in the last time I'd been in Mayanne's house. This time was different. I wasn't begging Owen to stay with me—for him to kiss me. But the memory was there. That first kiss, the first taste of the man who would get under my skin in a way that no one else ever had or ever would.

"Why don't you lie down?" She gestured to the bed that held so many memories it made my chest clench. Whether I wanted to admit it or not, I was changing. Intense emotions were becoming harder and harder to handle.

"Still don't believe you were destined for him?" Mayanne asked as she laid out several vials and a glass flask on the bedside table.

"I believe he's the most amazing man I've ever met."

"But you doubt destiny?"

"With everything looming over us, the only thing that seems destined is that we'll both get hurt."

"Stay confident. You will need it."

"That word has been thrown around a lot in the past few days."

"Because it's an important one." Mayanne smiled lightly.

"It's hard to feel that way right now." I ran my hand over the soft bedspread.

"You are still in control of your emotions. Don't forget that."

"Sometimes I am. Sometimes I'm not. I've had enough angry bursts and mood swings lately to prove it." I'd also manipulated a man again, and from Owen's reaction and the waiter's, I'd done it well.

"Then try harder to control them."

"You make it sound easy."

She laughed. "What in life is easy?"

"Not much apparently."

"Exactly. It all takes hard work, at least at times."

"Do you really think this is going to work?"

"Confidence, Daisy. Confidence."

"Oh no." I groaned.

"What?"

"Is this one of those things that is all in my head? Like it's not going to do anything except push me to fight against the change harder?" I'd read a lot about placebo sugar pills and things like that.

"Fighting it will help, but this should make the fight easier."

"What is it?"

"It's called a slug. It might make you sick, but it will also make the essence weaker."

"Great. I'm hoping it's called a slug because it slows

things down and not because it's gross."

"It's both actually, and I can tell you don't want to be sick or weaken the Allure essence."

"I want to weaken it, but I don't." I was attached to the new side of me though, even if it terrified me.

"It's already become a part of you."

"No." I shook my head. "I'm still human."

"You are human, mostly."

"I'm human." I was confident about that. Aside from my ridiculous mood swings, I was still me, bumbling along toward some sort of solution.

"Still don't trust me?"

"I trust you enough to let you do whatever it is you are going to do."

"I was right about Owen coming around."

"After I searched for him for years."

"But he came around, didn't he? I thought he was going to lose it when you told him to wait in the other room."

"He's protective, in a surprisingly nice way."

She rested her hand next to me. "Why surprisingly?"

"I don't usually go for those kind of guys. I mean, yeah, I loved that he saved me, but I don't need to be the damsel in distress again, you know?"

"I do. Drink this." She handed me a clear glass filled with a strange blue liquid that gave off a mist of smoke.

"What is it?" The blue color was one thing, but the smoke? Was it really safe to drink?

"It's strong. As I warned you, it will likely make you sick and you'll feel tired."

"You probably should have waited until after I finished the drink to remind me of those side effects."

She shrugged. "You deserve to know what's happening to you."

"I wish I did…"

"Violet has a plan. I know you're wary of her, and you have good reason, but I'd trust her."

"You think she's trustworthy?"

"Trustworthy enough, and she's your only option. Besides, if the change truly happens she's going to be the best one to help you."

I shivered. "I have to stop it in time."

"This should lengthen the window, but it won't work miracles. You are still going to have to work fast."

"Is this going to knock me out?" I moved around the glass in my hand.

"Quite possibly."

"If it does, will you have Owen come in?"

She smiled. "Absolutely. We won't let you out of our sight."

"Although I don't know what worse could happen to me—well, besides Owen disappearing again."

"He's not going anywhere. My guess is he's pacing outside the door."

"All right. I might as well get this over with." I closed my eyes and drank the pungent and sour tasting liquid. My stomach churned and I felt my gag reflex start, but I fought it down. It wouldn't do me any good if I threw it up. I'd have to drink it again.

I handed the empty glass to Mayanne and laid back against the pillow. "Ugh. I don't remember the last one tasting quite so bad."

"I guess I didn't warn you about the taste. That seemed

minor compared to the other side effects."

My stomach churned. "It's a one dose thing, right? I don't have to take another?"

"Only one. I'm afraid two would kill you… or at least the human part of you."

"Are Allures really immortal?" I opened my eyes.

"From everything I've heard, but I'd ask Violet that question."

"I don't want her to think that I was asking because I was ready to become one." The room started spinning and my head pounded, so I closed my eyes again.

"She knows you don't want to, and if my feeling is right, she doesn't want you to either. She cares about you in the only way an Allure can."

"You know a lot about Allures. More than anyone else I've met."

"I have a lot of free time. I've read a lot." She patted my arm. "How are you feeling?"

"Terrible. Beyond nauseous."

"It's what I figured would happen."

"Will it get better?"

"You'll get used to it, and eventually the sensation will fade completely."

"What happens when it fades completely?"

"It means you're almost out of time," her voice was nearly inaudible.

"So I should embrace the terrible sensation?"

"I do have one thing that might help. Of course it also might make it worse."

"What is it?" I asked nervously. I wasn't sure I could handle another concoction.

"I'll be right back."

I opened my eyes. "You're leaving?"

"I'll be less than a minute."

I waited anxiously, and finally she appeared holding something that appeared to be a sweatband. "What is that? If I didn't know any better I'd think it was a motion sickness bracelet."

"It is a motion sickness bracelet."

"That's your great idea?"

"It could help with the nausea." She put it around my wrist.

"I really hope it works."

"You and me both."

"You worried I won't be happy with your services?"

"I want you to make it to wherever it is you need to go. I want you to stay human. Mate with Owen. Have the life you want."

"Are you sure you've learned everything from books?" It didn't seem like she was all that surprised Allures were still around.

"We're all entitled to our secrets, Daisy. Don't you think?"

"In theory."

"You of all people should understand that life doesn't always work out the way we plan."

"I definitely do." I locked eyes with hers. "You can tell me, you know. I can keep a secret."

"Get better, reverse your change, and come back. We can celebrate and share stories."

"Okay." It wasn't my place to push her. It wasn't fair after all she had done for me.

She patted my hand. "Give yourself some time to rest. I

can send Owen in if you want."

I shook my head. "No. If he sees me like this he's going to freak out."

"Yet you wanted me to get him if you blacked out?"

"That would have been different. I need to deal with this myself. Find my own strength."

"That's the right idea, but don't forget it's okay to rely on a little bit of his strength too."

"A little bit sure, but this is going to take a lot."

She nodded. "I do have one more idea."

"Oh yeah?"

"Does any food appeal to you?"

"My stomach is doing flips." I put a hand on my upset stomach.

"I know, but does anything sound good?"

"Chocolate chip cookies." They always sounded good.

"Perfect. I happen to have some cookie dough waiting in the freezer."

"For real?"

"Don't act so surprised. I have a sweet tooth."

"How did you know I'd be craving something?"

"This isn't my first rodeo."

"You've dealt with someone else becoming an Allure?" I sat up with a start. That changed things. She knew more than she was saying.

"Not this exact situation, but I know what this type of potion does to a person."

"I need a few minutes, and I'll be fine."

"Should I go work on those cookies?"

"Sure. I'll wait here."

"You know he's going to want to come in."

"Fine." I struggled to sit up. My body ached, and I was overwhelmed with exhaustion.

Mayanne quickly helped prop me up with pillows. "I'll let him know you're ready to see him."

"Thanks." I struggled to come up with the words to sum up my gratitude. "For everything." I hoped she knew what I was really trying to say. That I was in debt to her.

"Of course. I'm sorry this happened to you, but maybe in the end it will be worth it. If you can step up to the challenge and fix things, you'll get your happily ever after."

"I'll settle for a happily for now."

She smiled. "You must be feeling better. You're making jokes."

"It's all this talk about cookies. It's amazing what the thought of baked goods can do to a person."

"I'm on it." She patted my leg before leaving the room and closing the door behind her.

Within seconds the door burst open. "Are you okay?" Owen ran over to the bed.

"I've been better, but I'm fine. Mayanne is making me cookies."

"I heard. Should I take it as a good sign that you have an appetite?"

"I need to get the bad taste out of my mouth." I downplayed how I really felt. There was no reason to worry him needlessly. It would only upset him, and he'd take it out on Violet and Hugh. If I was going to be with the three of them, I didn't want to give them any more reason to fight.

Owen put a hand on my forehead.

"Are you checking for a fever?"

He smiled. "Maybe."

"This stuff is supposed to help, not hurt."

"The important words are 'supposed to'. We knew there was a risk involved."

"I trust Mayanne. If the risk was too great she wouldn't have given it to me."

"You know I trust her. I brought you here the first time..."

"I know." I patted the bed. "We've returned to the scene."

"We have." He sat down beside me, stretching his long legs out next to mine.

"That was an amazing kiss."

It was. He brushed his lips against my cheek.

I took his hand in mine. "We've had other good kisses, but I'll never forget that one."

"That makes two of us." His lips moved to meet mine.

I pressed my lips against his, ignoring my slight headache and upset stomach.

He kissed me back harder, wrapping his arms around me. The nausea started to dissipate as I soaked up his taste.

I needed him, and I buried my hands in his hair. He cradled my head while his tongue pushed into my mouth. I forgot all about the potion and my discomfort as he deepened the kiss.

The door opened, and we broke the kiss.

"Sorry to interrupt." Levi stood in the doorway with an expression that said it all. He wasn't sorry. I guess a king doesn't need to be.

Owen groaned. "You always have impeccable timing."

"I have to keep you on your toes." His eyes twinkled with amusement. He enjoyed making Owen uncomfortable, but I sensed it wasn't in a bad way.

"Is there something you needed?" Owen leaned up on

his elbows.

"Violet wants to talk to Daisy."

"We'll be ready to talk to her in a few minutes."

Levi leaned a hand on the doorframe. "You know as well as I do she doesn't want you as part of the conversation."

"And you think that's okay?" Owen sat up. "I'm seriously supposed to leave Daisy to talk to Violet alone?"

"I think that's really up to Daisy to decide." Levi smiled sympathetically. "I know stepping aside isn't easy, but none of this is going to be easy."

"Would you quit sounding so wise all the time?" Owen moved off the bed. "I'm supposed to be the wise one keeping you in line." He laughed.

"Oh, how the tables have turned." Levi smirked.

"I might as well get this over with." I stood and straightened out my dress. "Where is she?"

"Waiting downstairs in the sitting room."

"Are the cookies ready yet?" Might as well get to the important questions.

Levi laughed. "They're in the oven."

"Great." I hadn't craved food in a while. It was a nice change of pace.

"I'll walk you down." Owen ran a hand through his hair as though he were checking that it wasn't messy.

"Thanks." I smiled. I knew I needed to talk to Violet alone, but I was glad Owen would still be close. I didn't want to rely on him, but that didn't mean I couldn't enjoy being with him.

Levi moved out of the doorway and led the way back to the stairs.

"There you are." Violet beamed when I reached the

bottom of the stairs.

"Finally acknowledging me?" She'd barely recognized my existence when we first walked in.

"Hey, it was your henchman giving me a hard time." She nodded toward where Owen and Levi flanked me, probably proving her point.

"Henchman?" Owen put a hand to his chest. "Try boyfriend."

"Boyfriend? How completely adorable." Hugh walked over.

I stood at the bottom of the stairs. "Where did you want to talk?"

"Outside?" she suggested.

"Sure." Fresh air sounded nice. Owen had helped the nausea, but it was still there. Maybe it would also help pass the time while I waited for the cookies.

"I'll be right here." Owen's eyes backed up his words. He wanted me to know that even if he was giving me space, he was still there if I needed him.

I nodded to let him know I understood before following Violet out into the hot early afternoon sun.

"You don't look good." She barely waited until the front door closed behind us before jumping in.

"Gee, nice to see you too." I hopped up onto the porch railing right next to a post so I could hold on.

"You know what I mean." She watched me carefully. "Are you ill?"

"I've been ill for a while."

"What did Mayanne give you?"

"I assumed you knew. All I know is it was something to slow down the change."

"Your body is craving emotions. You need to manipulate."
She leaned back against the rail next to me.

"I have plenty of emotion." I thought about the plethora
of emotions that had been swirling through me earlier lying
on the bed with Owen.

"You're going to have to give in. You'll feel better."

"And I'll lose more of myself. It's not worth the risk." It
would never be. I refused to give up my humanity until I had
absolutely no choice.

"How have you been doing?" she rested her hand
between us. Her nails had grown longer.

"Is this question different from the last one?"

"I'm asking more broadly." She tapped her nails.

"I'm scared, an emotional basket case, and…" I glanced
over my shoulder to make sure no one was nearby. It was
probably pointless, half the people we were with had super
hearing. "And the only thing that levels me out is intimacy
with Owen."

Violet grinned. "I can think of worse things for you to
have to do."

"I agree, but I can't spend my whole life having sex with
him."

"No… not every second of it."

"So what's the plan? Everyone seems to think you have
one."

"We get to Mount Majest. See the Elders."

"The Elders who you don't think are actually going to
help." Very reassuring.

"You never know. They like me."

"What aren't you saying?"

"You are already more perceptive." She straightened and

moved so she was standing in front of me.

"I guess it comes with the territory." I struggled to keep my head up. "But spit it out."

She looked off into the distance and didn't say anything. I decided to wait. Violet wasn't going to talk until she was ready. "You might not like what they have to say."

"Meaning they could refuse to help."

"Meaning any help they give will be on their own terms. Not yours."

Her words sunk in. Their terms may not be good for everyone around. "I need you to promise me something." I still didn't know everything about Violet, but she struck me as someone who would stick to her word.

"What is it?" She carefully avoided promising anything until she knew more. I tried to do the same thing.

"Promise me you won't let Owen get hurt."

"He's likely to get hurt whether you become an Allure or not."

"That's what I was afraid of."

"But I will do what I can. There are different types of hurt." She looked into the forest line.

On instinct I turned and followed her gaze. "Is something out there?"

"No, but you can never be too safe."

A chill ran through me. "Are you worried about someone watching me or you?"

"Either or both. There are always eyes in our world."

"Should we be doing more to protect ourselves? Have Owen check or something?" I was paranoid enough already. Now I was going to be checking over my shoulder every few minutes.

Lust

"It's not going to change a thing. When you've lived as long a life as I have, you begin to understand that some things are worth expending energy on and others are not."

"And helping me stop the change is worth your energy?" I still didn't know what to think. For a girl who couldn't feel, Violet seemed to be very concerned with what happened to me.

"Yes. It's worth it."

"How come you sometimes feel?" My filter was nearly gone.

"Haven't we gone over this before? I don't feel in the way you do."

"But you can sometimes..." I thought over our conversation with Myrtle. About Violet looking sad.

"Spit it out, Daisy. Is there something you want to ask me?" She crossed her arms, and it was an action that didn't fit her at all.

"What happened at the Applerose Gala?"

"I don't know what you are talking about." She looked out into the open field again.

"Yes you do. Why lie? You already know everything about me."

She blinked. "I'll say it again. I don't know what you are talking about."

"How can you expect me to trust you, if you don't trust me? Things don't work that way. There has to be some give and take."

"No." She moved in close. "That's not how it works. You want my help, I'm giving it. You want me to try to protect Owen, I'll try, but—"

"Fine. I'll stop pushing you, but please keep your promise.

He needs to survive. He needs to have a life. Happiness. Whether that's with or without me."

"Let's focus on getting to the Elders first. There's no reason to rush to a conversation we may not need to have."

"Fair enough. How are we getting there?" I wanted to know about the gala and that man, but pushing her wasn't going to help anything. I'd find out eventually. I didn't trust Violet completely, but I had no other choice. I had nowhere else to go.

"There are a few options."

"Which are?" Finally she was giving me some information.

"There are gates... that's the only way to reach Energo directly from here."

"Ok. Where are the gates?" The sooner we reached Energo, the better.

"Instead we can cut through another place first."

"Is there an advantage to this indirect way in?"

"We are less likely to be detected. That's a good thing." She stepped back.

"What's the catch? There has to be one."

"I know you're already nauseous. The trip isn't going to help matters any."

"Great."

"Somehow I don't think that band is going to be enough." She gestured to the motion sickness bracelet.

"Owen can come too." I wasn't actually asking a question. There was only one possibility I could accept.

"Yes. He's not going to let you go alone."

"His feelings are real." I needed Violet to understand even if it didn't change anything.

"I can tell."

"Mine are too." I hopped down off the railing.

"I can tell that too."

"I love him." Despite everything, I still knew that. I refused to let go of those feelings.

"I know."

"I want to love him always."

"Which is why I know you can handle the motion sickness."

"I know." I straightened up. Like it or not, I had no choice. "Do we have time to grab some cookies?"

Violet laughed. "There's always time for cookies."

"You like chocolate chip too?"

"Love them."

"At least that doesn't have to disappear as an Allure."

"It's a different kind of love though."

"I knew you were going to say that." I sighed. Everything was going to be different as an Allure. I wouldn't even enjoy cookies the same way anymore?

"I wanted to make sure you understood."

"I understand."

"Then let's go back inside." She started for the door, but then turned back. "I'm not all bad you know."

"I know. Why do you think I'm talking to you?"

"None of us are. Not Hugh, or Roland, or Louie. We're a product of what we've become."

"Heartless."

"No. Heartless isn't the right word." Violet locked her eyes with mine. "We have hearts."

"Then how would you describe it?"

"Frozen. Our hearts are frozen."

"No. That doesn't work."

"Why not?"

"Because a frozen heart can be thawed. What you are can't be fixed," I nearly whispered.

"Very true." She seemed unmoved by my words.

"But that doesn't bother you." The lack of feeling was still something I couldn't truly comprehend. How did you respond to anything or anyone without it?

"Sometimes it does, but it's less than you would think."

"Right now, does it?"

"My own condition doesn't, but yours does. I care about you as much as it's possible for me to care."

I believed her. Maybe I was naïve, but I needed to believe her to motivate myself to go along with whatever crazy plan she had. "And I appreciate that."

"But, Daisy?" She stopped right in front of the door.

"Yes?"

"When we're with the Elders, you might not believe that's true anymore, but remember it is. It will always be true."

"How do you know? How do you know it will always be true?"

"Because I do." She held open the door. "Let's get those cookies. It might help to get something in your stomach first."

"Unless that makes me sick."

"True. I guess you should make sure to enjoy them going down. It will make up for anything bad you experience with it coming back up."

"What's coming back up?" Owen stood just inside the doorway.

"Nothing." I didn't want to put the visual of me vomiting

cookies into his head.

"Did you two discuss everything necessary?" Owen looked between us.

"Pretty much. Now it's time for a snack before we get ready for our trip." I glanced toward the kitchen. The cookies smelled heavenly.

"To Energo?" Owen asked.

"Eventually." Violet started toward the kitchen. "But we've discussed it, and we're going to go in a roundabout way and make a stop. Make our entrance less conspicuous."

"What place are we making a stop at?"

"My home." Violet handed me a cookie.

nine

owen

"You expect us to walk through a tree to fairy land?" Levi spat out as we sat around the kitchen table.

"First of all, it isn't fairyland; second of all, I don't expect you to do anything. You're not invited." Violet took a small bite of her cookie.

"You can't tell me I'm not invited. I'm the king." Levi slammed his fist into the table.

Violet turned to Levi. "Yes, I realize you are the king here, but that doesn't mean anything where we're going."

"Unless someone else is given a territory, it's mine." Levi clenched his fist.

Violet rolled her eyes. "As I was saying, you will not be joining us."

"You can't tell me what to—"

"Who is going with you, Violet?" Georgina interrupted.

Violet smiled at Georgina. "Daisy has requested that Owen accompany us. Given the circumstances, I agree that he should come."

"Given the circumstances, I can come too." Levi glowered.

I needed to calm him down. "Levi, we have this. You need to take care of things here, and Allie and the kids need you."

"Let me send someone else with you then." He was worried. It took a lot to make him worried.

"No." Hugh shook his head. "It's bad enough that Romeo is coming."

"Don't call him that." Daisy set down her half eaten cookie. "The name implies we're star crossed lovers destined for a tragic end. That's not us."

Mayanne grinned. "Now there's the confidence we've all been waiting for."

Daisy picked at her cookie, creating a pile of crumbs. "How soon do we leave?"

Violet wiped her mouth with a napkin. "As soon as you're ready."

"We're ready." Daisy pushed back her chair.

"I can prepare bags for everyone." Georgina stood.

"I will make sure they both have everything they need." Violet nodded at Georgina. "I assure you they will be well attired."

"I'm not stealing more clothes." Daisy shook her head. "I know that's what you did in Colorado." Her voice was low, and there was no question she felt ashamed she even had the ability to do that.

"You really are a fighter." Violet's eyes gleamed with pride, as though Daisy's strength had something to do with her. "Too bad you don't want to become one of us."

"Here, at least change into the slacks Allie sent over."

Georgina stood. "I have those in the car. A girl should always dress her best, but she should also make sure to have alternatives."

"And there you have it. Expert advice." Levi grinned.

Georgina tried to hide a smile. "Leviathan please get my bag from the car."

"Of course." He walked outside.

Levi returned a moment later with the bag, and Daisy hurried off to change.

Violet pulled me to the side. "You need to keep yourself reined in over the next few days. We know you care about her, but that doesn't mean you should argue with me every chance you get. We need to work together to both get what we want."

"And what is it that you want?" I still didn't believe her motivations were as innocent as she pretended.

"It's mine to know."

I shook my head. "No, it's not. That's not good enough. We could be walking into a trap for all I know."

"You're not." She looked toward the doorway, probably checking for Daisy.

"And you expect me to take your word for it, just like that?"

"What other choice do you have?" Her eyes twinkled.

"Just level with me. What do you want from all this?"

"All you need to know is that it involves Daisy being happy and healthy. I do not wish her ill. I'd like to get her exactly what she wants, but if that's not an option, then I will take her under my wing and teach her everything she needs to know to become an Allure."

"Is that really your job?"

"Would you prefer Roland do it? Because he'd be the more natural one?"

"No. I don't want him near her." I clenched my teeth.

"It's not the kind of attraction Hugh made it sound like. It's the essence he's attracted to." Violet stood and stretched.

"Which means you kept him away because you're afraid of what he'll do."

"I'm afraid of what he'll try to stop us from doing." She rolled her shoulders.

"But if you get the essence back, can't you give it to someone else?"

"If we found the right person." Hugh pushed back his chair. "That isn't exactly easy."

"It's that hard?" I wasn't asking a question.

"Yes. Very. It might take decades. Possibly a century since it's a whole essence."

"And he doesn't want to wait that long."

"He's been unhappy for a while now. He's craving the companionship."

"Then he should make his own."

"And he will, but he wants his maker."

"She isn't his maker."

"No, she's not, but she feels like her. She also kind of looks like her."

"Now you mention that." I shook my head.

"Not in features exactly, just expressions. The way she holds herself. Maybe I have it wrong, maybe Daisy's changed to adapt to the essence." Violet held up her arms. "What do I know anyway?"

"No matter what happens we keep Daisy safe." That was the bottom line.

Violet glanced over her shoulder. "She wanted me to promise the same thing about you."

"And did you?"

"Well, her exact words were about worrying that you'd be hurt. I told her the truth. I told her if we failed, you'd be hurt."

"We're not going to fail. That's not an option at all." I stood. I couldn't sit around a moment more.

Hugh smirked. "Not an option, but a possibility. Failure is always a possibility, even for the strongest, and you aren't the strongest."

"Do you want to antagonize me?" I moved toward him.

"It's the truth. Although Daisy is one of the strongest beings I've ever met."

"She is." We agreed on something.

"Speaking of which." Violet gestured to the doorway.

I turned to see Daisy walk in wearing jeans and a fitted t-shirt. She looked perfect. She looked beautiful dressed up, but there was something about simple casual clothes that brought out her inner beauty even more. "Sorry about that. I had to talk to Mayanne a little bit more."

"It's fine. We've had a lovely chat." Violet picked up another cookie. "Still hungry?"

"Nope." Daisy shook her head. "Let's do this."

"Are you leaving?" Georgina and Levi strolled back into the room. They'd disappeared earlier, and I hadn't asked questions.

"Yes. There's no reason to hold off any longer," Daisy replied.

Georgina pulled her into a hug. "Best of luck on your journey."

Daisy stepped back in surprise. "Thank you."

Georgina nodded. "My bet is on you."

Daisy's eyes widened slightly. "I didn't take you as someone who bets."

"Everyone is entitled to her secrets." Georgina winked.

"Take care of Owen for me." Levi held out his hand to her.

"Of course." She accepted his hand and shook it. "I won't let anything happen to him."

"I know. He's in good hands."

I put an arm around her. "And I won't let anything happen to you either."

"Good." Mayanne smiled. "Daisy's a friend of mine. I'm protective of my friends."

"As you should be." Violet moved toward the doorway. Hugh pushed past her without a word.

"Where's Hugh going?" Daisy asked.

"Waiting outside. Goodbyes aren't his thing."

"Even when they are with people he doesn't care about?" Levi asked skeptically.

"What makes you think he doesn't care about any of you?" Violet teased.

"Be safe." Georgina spoke softly.

"We will do our best. Thanks for the hospitality." Violet turned back around.

"Thanks for the help, Levi." Hopefully I'd be able to repay him eventually.

"Anytime, man."

My relationship with Levi was complicated, but the bottom line was we were good friends. I knew Levi had my back when it counted.

"Just do me a favor. Come back when you're all done."

"I plan on it." I caught up with Daisy and Violet outside.

Hugh was already seated in the driver's seat of the SUV. Daisy and I slipped into the backseat.

"How did the goodbyes go?" Hugh slowly backed out of the drive.

"They went fine. I'm not sure why you hid out here." Daisy buckled her seatbelt.

"I had more important things to do."

"Oh yeah?"

"Yeah. We've got directions in the GPS." He pointed to the screen.

"You guys need directions?" Daisy leaned forward toward the front.

"No, but it seemed like something I should do."

Daisy shook her head. "You guys are weird."

Hugh looked at us in the rearview mirror. "Like you should talk?"

"How far are we driving?" They wanted to be secretive? Fine. They could at least tell us that.

"We need to get to Charleston."

"Charleston, South Carolina or West Virginia?" That would make a big difference in the driving time.

"South Carolina."

"So that's about 750 miles from here."

"Good guess."

"It's not a guess." I knew distances. I needed to know exactly how long it would take to get to any place in Levi's territory. So much of my life had been dedicated to preparing to be his advisor, yet I hadn't realized it at the time. I'd honestly been surprised when he'd appointed me. I was his friend, but politically there were better Pterons for the position. My family held no power. Or they didn't before. With Hailey and I both advisors now we were positioning ourselves to be one of the strongest families. I pushed the thought from my head. We weren't positioning ourselves to be anything. We were friends with the king and queen and that helped us get jobs. I'd abandoned my job. Hopefully Hailey didn't do the same thing because I wasn't sure what that would mean for the Kaye family's reputation.

Hugh drove us down the quiet country roads, past a large pond with an old covered bridge.

"I had a bridge like that near my house growing up." Daisy looked wistfully out the window.

"Did you also play with puppies and kittens?" Hugh laughed.

"Stop it, Hugh." Violet pushed his arm. "Cut Daisy a break."

"You are no fun."

"I'm not concerned with whether I'm fun."

Hugh shrugged. "Whatever."

I followed Daisy's lead and gazed out the window. I'd spent my whole life in Louisiana, yet I knew so little of the state outside New Orleans. It's funny how you can be so close to something, yet know it so little. Eventually the countryside was replaced with the interstate. We had a long trip ahead of us.

Daisy sighed, and I looked over. "Is everything okay?"

"I'm fine." She smiled lightly. "At least we have a plan."

"A plan that has to work." It was hard to have confidence in a plan you still didn't know that much about.

"It doesn't have to work," Hugh shot back.

"It does." I wasn't in the mood to argue with him. I wasn't in the mood to do anything but find a way to stop the change.

We stopped once for gas and food, but otherwise we drove straight through to Charleston. I spent the ride trying to figure out where we were really going, and trying to come up with every possible escape plan. I didn't want to trust the Allures, but we didn't have another choice. All I could do was take the word of Mayanne and Georgina. They had no reason to trick me, and I hoped they didn't have a hidden agenda.

"I haven't been here in years." Daisy looked out her window. She'd spent nearly the whole trip that way. I left her to her own thoughts. She'd have told me if she were interested in talking.

"To Charleston?" Violet asked.

"Yeah. I didn't grow up all that far from here, but since starting college I missed all the family trips." She put a hand on her stomach.

I cringed. I couldn't stand to see her in discomfort, and she was still feeling sick.

"We don't come all that often either." Hugh sounded surprisingly nice.

"Isn't this how you get to your home?"

"Yes, but we don't go home often. We find plenty of substitutes elsewhere."

"Like abandoned amusement parks." Daisy smiled.

"Yes."

"Abandoned amusement parks?" I raised an eyebrow.

"Yes. They were staying at the old amusement park in

99

New Orleans. The one that closed after Katrina."

"Oh... interesting." They had the ability to stay anywhere in the world they wanted, the finest hotels or homes, yet they choose an abandoned amusement park that had been under several feet of water?

Violet turned in her seat. "Don't judge it until you've seen it."

"It was pretty cool. Different, but cool." Daisy stretched. "I was skeptical at first, but they had a nice set up."

"By skeptical she means she expected us to kill her." Hugh laughed.

"How are you laughing?" Daisy pouted. "It was a completely reasonable thing to worry about considering the circumstances."

I loved that Daisy could see the potential in the abandoned park. Not many people could. It's not like she was an eternal optimist. She wasn't, but she could understand why people saw beauty in another person's trash.

"This home isn't like the amusement park though, is it?" Daisy rested her hand between us. "Not because I care, but..."

Violet turned back around. "You'll see for yourself in a few minutes."

"We're that close?" Daisy leaned forward.

"Weren't you the one who was in a hurry?" Hugh asked.

"Yes, but that doesn't mean I'm ready to face whatever is about to come my way."

Hugh continued down the two lane road lined with a mix of old and new buildings. It was one of those areas that had been built over time. He suddenly slowed and turned onto a dirt road. I was glad he'd chosen an SUV. "Angel Oak?"

I noted the sign. "I should have known."

"Tell anyone about it and you're dead, bird." Hugh didn't mince words.

"I can understand secrets. Pterons have more than a few of our own."

"What's Angel Oak?" Daisy asked over the noise from the uneven road below us.

"It's one of the oldest trees east of the Missisippi."

"Why's it called Angel Oak?" Daisy looked out at the dark night.

"Originally it comes from the name of some of the people who owned the land, but the angel name also works because people have reported seeing the ghosts of dead slaves here." Violet opened her window. "Now that's a time I'd never want to go back to."

"You were around before the civil war?" Daisy's eyed widened. "That's crazy."

"I was around long before that."

"Wow." Daisy leaned back against the seat.

"You're not that old, Violet." Hugh patted her leg.

"Yeah, not that old."

"No matter how hold you are, you look good for your age." I thought I'd break some of the tension.

Violet laughed. "Thanks. I appreciate that."

Hugh stopped the car in front of a tall chain-link fence. Large signs spelled out the hours for the park. We were clearly outside of them.

We got out slowly. We were all in a hurry, yet not. Although we were in a rush to find answers for Daisy, the journey didn't seem particularly enjoyable.

"We're not supposed to take you through this way."

Violet spoke calmly.

"But you're going to anyway." Daisy closed her eyes.

"Yes. I really don't care about the rules anymore."

"Please tell me you're not on a suicide mission." That thought had already occurred to me, but I really hoped it wasn't real.

"No. Not a suicide mission."

"It's closed right now, huh? You guys like breaking into places when they are closed." Daisy looked all around her.

"We aren't breaking in here. It's ours. We just can't use it when tourists are around." Violet hesitated with her hand on the door handle.

"Gotcha."

"Please tell me you're going to return this car." Daisy made no motion to move once Hugh parked.

"Why are you always so concerned with people getting their cars back?" Hugh studied her.

"Because people pay hard earned money for their cars," she answered immediately. I knew it was for the same reason she cared so much about upsetting Allie. She had a guilt complex. I knew the feeling. I'd occasionally suffered from one myself.

"It's just an item." Hugh pushed the door open. "All items can be replaced."

"Only if you have the money to replace them."

"But they can be replaced." He got out and went right over to the chain-link fence. He effortlessly scaled the fence and landed on the other side.

Violet got out to follow, but then leaned back in. "What he's trying to say is that you should worry less about people's things and more about people."

"But you guys mess with people too." Daisy got out and slammed her door. I hurried out through my side.

"We don't hurt them."

"Of course you do!" She threw up her hands. I didn't immediately move to calm her down. She had every right to say her piece. "You hurt people by getting them in trouble with the people they care about, by taking things from them, by making them feel or think things that aren't really their thoughts or feelings. That hurts them."

Violet pressed her lips together. "We do what we have to do in order to survive. That's all we can do."

"There has to be another way." She walked toward the fence.

"We'll see what tune you are singing—"

"Enough!" Violet glared at Hugh through the chain link. "We need to move. No more arguing."

"I'll second that." I'd held back so Daisy wouldn't feel like I was trying to get involved in all her fights, but arguing about whether Allures hurt people or not would do absolutely nothing in the effort to keep her human.

"Agreed." Daisy touched the fence. "Do we really have to climb a chain-link fence again?"

"You did fine with it last time, what's the problem?" Violet scaled the fence.

"I'm glad I changed into pants."

Hugh laughed. "Think a dress would get in your way?"

She didn't answer. "Let's get this over with." She climbed up and over.

Violet was right. Daisy had no trouble scaling the fence. I followed closely behind, choosing not to use my wings in case there were security cameras. It would be easier to get our faces deleted from the footage than to explain a giant set of wings.

I joined Daisy inside the fence and walked with her toward the giant oak tree.

She gazed up at it. "Beautiful."

The tall tree was beautiful. Its most striking feature were its low branches that stretched out in every direction and seemed to go on forever. There was something surreal about the tree.

"It's been here for over four hundred years." Violet stood right next to it. "It's grown a lot, but it's still the same tree."

"Were you around when it was planted?" I asked.

"Didn't you hear Georgina?" Violet wagged her finger in the air. "You never ask a woman's age."

Hugh laughed. "I don't know why you are so hesitant to tell them your story, Violet. It's a good one."

"Why don't you tell them yours, huh, Hugh? If telling stories is of so little consequence."

He paled. "My story isn't nearly as interesting as yours."

"What's Roland's?" Daisy asked.

"It's his to tell." Violet touched one of the low hanging branches. "This is the part that is going to make you nauseous."

"Touching the tree?"

"Traveling through it."

"We're really traveling through a tree?" Daisy's eyes widened. "You have got to be kidding me."

"With everything else going on, it's the tree travel you can't accept?"

"I can accept it in theory. I just can't believe we're going to do it."

"You are both going to have to close your eyes." Hugh put his hands behind his head. I couldn't tell if he was stretching or flexing his muscles.

I ignored his display. "Why?"

"Because tree travel isn't for humans or Pterons. It's meant only for us."

"And I'm practically an Allure." Daisy put a hand on her hip.

"But practically doesn't mean anything. You're still human."

She rolled her eyes. "I'll close my eyes, but this had better not be a joke where you pretend we've been transported someplace but in reality we haven't moved at all."

"I wouldn't worry about that." Violet strode toward the tree. "I guarantee you're going to feel it."

"Why?" Daisy asked with alarm. "Does it make you sick?"

"Slightly."

"Really?" I wanted to make sure she wasn't messing with Daisy.

"Why are you surprised?" Violet watched me with curiosity. She seemed to like to study our responses.

"I'm surprised you'd subject yourself to something unpleasant. You can avoid anything you don't like."

She gently touched the trunk of the tree. "It's one of the only way to get back home."

"When we close our eyes, what happens?" Daisy slipped her hand into mine.

"We touch the tree and touch you guys. We all travel."

"How do I know you won't leave me behind?" She'd been almost too willing to bring me along with them. It made me suspicious.

"Because you're holding hands. She's not going anywhere without you."

"So you say."

"At this point, you are going to have to take our word for it."

"I'm tired of people saying things like that." I was used to being in control.

"Join the club." Daisy leaned into my side.

Violet glanced up at the dark sky. "We need to do this."

"Fine." Daisy shut her eyes. "We're ready."

I closed my eyes and felt the ground begin to shake underneath us. I held onto Daisy's hand as tightly as I could. I tried to open my eyes, but I couldn't. It was as though gravity was pushing down on us at ten times the usual force. My body felt inside out, my ears, nose, mouth, and eyes burned, and I needed it to be over. The shaking died down, and it was replaced by the sudden sensation of falling. I felt sick to my stomach, and I worried about Daisy. She'd been sick even before this experience.

Before I could fully process it, our bodies made contact with the ground.

"Ouch!" Daisy cried.

"You okay?" I opened my eyes to find her sprawled out next to me. I still held her hand in mine.

"Is it over?" She blinked rapidly, still lying down.

I sat up. We were on a sandy beach lying underneath a palm tree. I had no way to know how far away we were from Angel Oak.

"Violet?" I called out. A seemingly endless mass of dark blue water stood on one side of us, while a thick jungle stood behind.

"Where are they?" Daisy sat up, and I helped her to standing.

"I don't know." This was great. Fantastic. They'd transported us to some unknown place and dumped us.

"Where did they go?" She glanced around. "There's no way they ditched us."

"Right now it looks like they did." I wanted to be positive for her, but realism was more likely to help us out of our current situation. "First things first. We have to figure out where we are."

"You make that sound easy." She dusted off her pants.

"We may only be a few miles away from where we started. Violet might have been making the whole transporting to another realm stuff up." We'd definitely moved though. We were on a beach and not one I recognized.

"Do you really believe that?" Daisy gazed out at the dark water. "This doesn't look like the Charleston beaches I remember, and look at that." She pointed up at the sky.

"It's the most logical answer." I followed Daisy's gaze and noticed an odd glowing red ball of light set in the darkening sky.

"What is that?" She pointed.

"Your guess is as good as mine."

"Do we wait here or start exploring?"

I needed to come up with a plan and fast. Daisy was relying on me. I'd put my trust in the hands of the wrong people, and now we were wasting time. Maybe that was Violet's plan all along. She wanted to distract us so we couldn't stop the change in time.

Before I could formulate anything useful I heard

something moving in the jungle behind us. I grabbed hold of Daisy's hand.

"You heard that too?" she asked nervously.

I nodded. "Unfortunately, I did."

"Maybe it's just a squirrel."

"Could be." I doubted it. I had great senses. I always knew what was going on around me, but I couldn't place it this time. I didn't recognize what it was. Something was messing with me. Nothing felt normal, I was turned around.

The shuffling got louder, and it was joined by loud laughter. It was cackling that started in one spot, but then it continued all around us. We were surrounded.

"What's going on?" Daisy trembled beside me. "Is this a joke or something?"

I turned so my back faced away from Daisy, but I held on to her hand. I transformed, allowing my large black wings to rip through my t-shirt.

I felt the familiar surge of strength as I fully transformed. I could handle anything that came our way. I'd protect Daisy no matter what happened.

"Look, we made him mad," a tiny voice called out. "He has his wings out."

"And his eyes are black."

I hadn't realized how complete my transformation was. I needed to hold onto my human side somewhat with Daisy close by.

A petite girl with a pale complexion and wild red hair walked into the clearing. She held her hands out in front of her. "We won't hurt you."

"Where are we?" I tried to stay calm, but my Pteron side was in full attack mode. If it weren't for the girl's small size it would have been worse. I was nearly certain she was some sort of Dryad, and they weren't known to be violent, but I wasn't willing to put my guard down.

The laughter grew louder.

"Hello. Could you stop laughing and tell us what's going on?" Daisy sounded so calm and collected. I was impressed.

The laughing stopped, and at least a dozen people walked out of the woods from around us. They were all dressed in green tunics and brown pants. Although their skin tones varied, each one of them had the same shock of red hair that fell around them in wild waves. The Dryads I knew weren't all quite so wild looking, but that's what they had to be.

Daisy cleared her throat. "Uh hi. We're lost and are looking for some friends."

"You are an Allure?" One of the girls walked toward Daisy. "I haven't seen a new one in years."

"No. I'm hum—" Then she seemed to think better of it. "Do you know Violet and Hugh?"

"They were taken by the Force."

I wasn't sure what the Force was exactly, but I had a hunch. "The police force?"

The girl nodded. "Yes, but no one calls them police now. They're just the Force."

"Okay, but when were they taken? We were with them a few minutes ago." I checked our surroundings. Hugh and Violet were nowhere to be seen.

"When they were transported. There was a bounty on their head." A male explained.

"A big one." The first girl to enter the clearing nodded. "Biggest I have ever heard of."

"A bounty?" Were Violet and Hugh in trouble? Why

would they have returned home then?

"The announcement gave no reasons."

"This makes no sense." Daisy dug her foot into the damp soil. "None of this makes sense.

"My bet is you're going to have a bounty on your head too. You brought a Pteron into the Glamour Realm." She pointed a thumb at me.

"I had a good reason to bring him," she looked at me for help. "A good reason."

I thought fast. "I'm escorting her home by order of The Society."

"I thought you were with Violet and Hugh?" The male asked suspiciously.

"We were, but I was still her escort."

"She's been escorted. You may leave." He moved his hand as if to shoo me away.

"He can't leave yet." Daisy squeezed my hand. "We have other reasons to be here."

"Do you?" The girl asked. "This should be interesting."

ten

daisy

What kind of mess were we in now? It was bad enough that Violet wanted to take us through some weird other world to get to Mount Majest, but now we were on our own, and both of us might be in trouble. What would happen if, or more likely when, these people discovered I wasn't an Allure? Things were only going to get worse.

"What other business does he have here?" The girl asked again. I'd put my foot in my mouth, but I had to say something. Otherwise one of them might make him leave. Owen was strong, but who knew what these people could do?

"It's private." I tried to keep my voice firm. "Do you know how we can find Violet and Hugh? I know you said they're in some sort of trouble, but maybe we can help."

"Are you suffering from memory loss?" The first girl walked over. Owen started to move in front of me, but I stopped him. She wasn't going to hurt me. She put her hands

111

on either side of my head. "You're not full Allure yet, huh? That's the problem. Is this your first time in the Glamour Realm?"

"Yes." Change of plans. Maybe playing on my lack of knowledge could be a help rather than hindrance.

"That changes things." Something silent passed between the two.

The guy nodded and walked toward me. "What does it change? She's still breaking the rules."

"Not intentionally…" The girl rested her chin in her fisted hand. "Clearly Hugh made her before he could tell her."

The guy shook his head. "There's no way Hugh made her."

"Why not?" the girl asked.

"It's a completely different essence. It's…." His eyes darkened. "It's Taylor."

"How could that be?" The once friendly girl stepped back. The others instantly looked suspicious. "She's been missing… and this girl isn't her."

I shook my head. "It's not like that. A witch… it wasn't my fault."

Several more of the people stepped closer.

"Honestly, it wasn't my fault."

Owen glared at the crowd, and they stopped. "Just tell them the truth."

"The truth?" The angry guy asked.

"Yes. The truth. Roland made Daisy." Owen pulled me against his side. "Roland was made by Taylor."

"Oh." The girl sighed with relief. "Where is he?"

"I don't know. Violet and Hugh were helping." I went along with the story. It was easier and hopefully safer that way.

"You poor thing." The first girl hugged me in an awkward way since Owen wasn't budging. "Separated from your maker before you even understand the way of things."

"That doesn't explain why she's with him." The angry guy scowled. "She still hasn't told us the truth about that."

"I already told you. I'm her protection. The king assigned me to guard her until she found her maker. That was the secret. We had no idea there were still Allures around and now that we do; it's our duty to make sure no harm comes to this new one."

"The Society has changed…" The angry guy seemed lost in thought. "Do you have any idea where Roland might be?"

"With the Elders." I had to risk sharing the information. It was the only clue I had, and if there was any chance these people could lead us there, I had to take the chance.

Several of them gasped. "Has he been summoned there?"

I hated lying, but what could I do? "Possibly. Do you know how to find them?"

"We can find the Elders, but that doesn't mean they will see you." The girl crossed her arms. "You are not even a full Allure after all."

"I need to find him." Then I thought of something. "Does the Force work with the Elders? Is that where Violet and Hugh would have been brought?"

The girl shook her head. "No. The Force is its own separate entity. ." She held out her hand. "I'm Sky by the way. Who are you?"

"Daisy." We were lying about so much already. I decided using my real first name could be helpful.

"Nice name." The angry guy held out his hand. "I'm

Adrian."

I accepted the surprisingly firm handshake. "Nice to meet you."

I waited as half a dozen more introduced themselves. No one moved to introduce themselves to Owen, so I took care of that myself. "This is Owen."

"Hi," they mumbled before turning back to me. "You are just in time for the Blood Moon Festival."

"The what?" Owen and I looked at each other.

"The Blood Moon. It's exactly what it sounds like. A festival dedicated to the blood moon."

"That red thing?" I pointed into the sky.

"Yes. It's our blood moon. It only comes once a year."

"Oh. Good timing I guess." Or bad. Maybe they had a festival to appease negative things. Hopefully there was no sacrifice involved.

"You're Dryads." Owen shook hands with the girl. "I've met some of your kind."

"The Dryads of your world are nothing like us." She crinkled up her nose.

"Why not?" he asked.

"Because they gave up most of their power. They left their home realm."

"And you get power from your home realm?" I asked.

"Yes. From our trees of course." She crossed her arms.

I filed away that information for later. "We wouldn't want to impose on your celebration. If you could send us in the direction we need to go, we'll be out of your way."

"Having an Allure at our festival would be an honor." One of the girls, I was pretty sure her name was Donna said.

"Even a new Allure who's just now changing?" I still

wasn't sure what my standing was.

"Of course. We'd love to have you come." Adrian smiled.

"I need to keep Owen with me."

"He can come if he behaves." Adrian narrowed his eyes.

Owen glowered. "Dryads answer to the king where I come from."

"But you're not where you come from. We don't answer to any king here."

"Who is the leader then?" I asked.

"The Elders of course. Isn't that why you want to find them?"

"Yes, but I thought maybe there was something on the local level." I was grasping at straws. I was in so over my head it wasn't funny.

"Are you hungry?" Donna asked Owen.

He shook his head. "Thank you, but I'm fine."

"We have plenty of food in the village. Why don't you come with me?" She beamed up at him.

He smiled, but moved closer to my side. "I'm staying with Daisy."

"She's going to be fine right here."

"We stay together." I wasn't giving in on that. This time it wasn't for my own security. It was for Owen's. Who knew what would happen to him? He was incredibly strong, but I had absolutely no idea what these creatures were capable of, and we were severely out numbered.

Donna smiled at me. "Are you hungry too? Do you still have an appetite?"

"Not much of one, but Allures can still eat." I'd seen Allures eating several times.

"They can, but usually they are picky. Our simple foods

don't usually appeal."

"I like simple." I had always been the least picky of all my friends and family.

"Then you're still human. You won't want simple later."

"Not every Allure is the same." Violet and Hugh were completely different from one another.

"No, but simplicity isn't in your makeup. You like grander things, which is fine by us. We all have our place."

"It doesn't matter. Owen needs to eat, so I'll come with him." I was tired of this conversation.

"I have a better idea." Sky popped up on her toes. "Want to see Roland's house?"

"His house?" Violet must have been literal when she said she'd take us to her home. Or not. She had ditched us the second we arrived, unless the Dryads were to be believed, and they'd been transferred to the Force.

"Yes. Maybe that would be the best way to find him. I doubt he's with the Elders. No one stays on Mount Majest long. You either get an audience or you don't."

"Daisy and I are staying together," Owen interrupted. "I'm not hungry. We can go to the house first."

"But then you won't see our festival." Donna's face fell.

"How far away is his house?" Owen asked. "Can't we do both?"

"In theory, yes."

"In theory?" I was still trying to figure out what to do. I'd been told over and over again that the Elders wouldn't see me if I simply showed up, so maybe finding Roland would help too, especially if we couldn't find Violet and Hugh. The Dryads had gotten strange when Taylor came up. Was it only because she was a missing Allure, or was there more?

Something told me finding out would be important.

"You're going to get distracted, and he'll never come back." Donna looked down at the ground.

"Why do you care so much whether he goes to your festival?" I sized up the tiny Dryad.

"Because we never get non-fairies here."

"So? You like him because he's exotic or something?"

Owen laughed under his breath.

"What about you? Why are you with him?"

"Because I—" I stopped. An Allure couldn't love. I had to be careful. "Because he's protecting me."

Adrian smiled reassuringly. "The change is making you emotional, but don't let Donna get to you. If she bothers you, hope that you never meet a Nymph."

"Nymphs? They really exist?" I remembered the name of the mythological creature from school. Unless I was mistaken they were also the source of the modern day term "nympho."

"Oh, yes." Owen nodded.

"And you know them?"

He held up his hands as though in defense. "Not in any of the ways you're thinking."

"Are you sleeping with Roland?" Sky asked.

I coughed. "Uh, no."

"Really? That happens a lot."

"Not with us."

"But Allures like sex."

"Don't most people like sex?" I was going to lose my temper if we didn't start moving soon. Why did these Dryads keep moving the conversation in circles? It was as though they were purposely sabotaging us. Maybe they were.

117

"Yes, but you guys mostly live through other people's emotions. Sex is supposedly still good though. I guess the physical feelings are real." Adrian smiled.

"Great." I glanced all around me. I'd have left if I had an inkling of what direction to go.

"Where's Roland's house?" Owen shared my impatience.

"I'll take you," Adrian offered. "I need to go that way anyway."

"I'm coming too." Both girls said at once.

"Or you could just tell us the general direction." The sooner we ditched these Dryads the better as far as I was concerned, and it wasn't only because of Donna. I didn't trust any of them. I didn't trust anyone but Owen anymore. Mayanne had been so insistent I trust Violet. Look at how far that got us. What if the paste she gave me had been fake? Maybe it had only been an attempt to slow me down.

I sighed. I couldn't afford to follow that train of thought. I needed to find information on Taylor and somehow use that to gain an audience with the Elders. Whether her fault or not, Violet wasn't with us. Owen and I were on our own.

"You'll never find it alone." Adrian rolled up the sleeves of his green tunic.

"You want to see Panna. She doesn't want to see you." Sky grinned.

Adrian huffed. "Panna has nothing to do with it."

"No? You just happen to want an excuse to go into the Allure village?" Sky ribbed.

I caught Owen's eye. Was it time we cut our losses and searched for it ourselves? "Allure village? There is actually a place called the Allure Village?"

"Did you think they lived with the rest of us?" Donna

shook her head.

Sky touched Donna's arm and something silent passed between them. "The Allures are kind of in charge here."

"Hasn't Roland told you anything?" Adrian asked.

"No. He's told me nothing." He hadn't, but then again it wasn't his job. It was no one's job because I didn't have a maker.

"And Violet didn't either?" he asked.

"She was supposed to, and then we got separated." Or ditched. I still didn't know which one it was.

He nodded, as if in understanding. "We could take you to her house too."

"Yes. She actually said she wanted us to go there."

"Great. Let's go then." Sky grinned. "You'll find both in the village."

"Good." Owen retracted his wings. "What direction are we going in?"

"This way." Sky started skipping across the glade.

eleven

daisy

I wanted to laugh. I needed to laugh as I watched this tiny pixie of a girl frolicking across the meadow, but I couldn't. They may have been little, but something told me they weren't the kind of creatures you wanted to anger. I guess you never wanted to make any creatures mad. Life was so much simpler when I only knew about humans. But it was all worth it. I looked over at Owen. It was all worth it because I'd met him.

We'd been keeping our hands to ourselves, I figured letting the Dryads know we were involved wasn't a good thing. I was beginning to understand Allures didn't get involved with anyone else. The whole not being able to feel emotion thing probably played a huge role in that.

Sky led the way through the lush meadow. Every so often a bird swooped through the sky near us, but otherwise it was quiet enough I could hear the wind move through the grass. Well, aside from Donna talking. We walked for at least a mile before we reached another forest.

"I have always wanted to fly. You are incredibly lucky." Donna prattled on to Owen. She'd been chatting him up the whole walk.

"Flight is great, but I'm sure being a Dryad has its benefits." Owen glanced up at the red moon. I'd been doing the same thing myself. It was a reminder we were far from home.

I took a few deep breaths, Owen was only being polite. He wasn't flirting. I'd never been a jealous person before, but now I couldn't even hold myself together. I needed to calm down before I got us into even more trouble than we were already. An Allure wasn't supposed to be in love.

"Ignore her." Sky fell back to walk next to me. "She's just excited."

"I was making sure she didn't distract him from his job."

"His job of protecting you?" She leaned in. "You don't need protection here."

"I thought I was going to be in trouble. I think I do need protection."

"His kind of protection isn't going to help you with the Force. It could only hurt."

"But I want him here anyway."

"Listen, you are still human sort of?" Her eyes were kind. "Yes."

"Then do the right thing."

"Which is?" I didn't actually want to hear the answer because I was afraid of what it would be.

"Send him back home. Give him a chance."

"He has a chance here. We're both going home." I clenched my fists together at my side. From jealousy to anger. My emotions were boiling up and mixing together in a somewhat painful way.

"You already know you want to leave the Glamour Realm? You want to live with the humans?"

"I'm from the human world."

"So? It's not like you are going to care about anyone there anymore." Her words weren't cruel, they were purely a statement of fact, but they clawed at me in a way that made my emotions more confusing.

She was wrong. That couldn't be possible. Mom. Her face flashed through my head again. I'd been so focused on my feelings for Owen I hadn't been thinking about everyone else in my life. No way. I wasn't losing that feeling of warmth that coursed through me every time I pictured my mother's face or her voice. Or the way my father could crack me up, or my brother could simultaneously annoy me yet make everything so much more fun. "I'm going back."

"You can say what you want to say now. You won't be saying it soon."

"How did you know I was Allure?" The Pterons didn't know, so it wasn't obvious to all paranormal creatures. But maybe that was because most of them hadn't met an Allure before.

"It's obvious. True nature types can always tell." She clasped her hands in front of her.

"Is an Allure a nature type?" Violet hadn't told me anything about what an Allure *was*, only what they did.

"No. They are a type all of their own. Well, you are. I shouldn't talk as though you aren't one of them." She straightened up. "They are not tied to the land or anything in nature."

I wasn't one, and I wouldn't be I reminded myself so I wouldn't fall to the floor in despair. The possibility of stopping the change was the only thing that kept me moving. "But they live in your realm."

"They predate all of us," Sky puffed out her chest.

"Oh." I glanced over at Owen. He was still deep in conversation with Donna. Perfect.

"And the Allures all descend directly from the gods." She picked up her pace.

I hurried to keep up. "People keep saying that, but I don't understand."

"I'm not the one to explain it."

"Great. Another question to wait for an answer to. " My shoulders slumped.

Out of the corner of my eye I watched her studying me. "Did you know what you were agreeing to when you accepted the gift? Did you consider what you would lose?"

I shook my head without thinking.

"That's a capital crime."

"What is?"

"Changing someone without giving proper information."

"But I wasn't changed. Well, not in the way you're supposed to be." I couldn't keep up the ruse anymore. I was going to get everyone hurt. A capital crime? Roland didn't deserve that.

"Wait. Before Owen interrupted you were talking about a witch. What did you mean?"

So she had picked up on that. "Forget it. Just know Roland did nothing wrong."

"You are lying about everything."

I looked down. "I don't know what's true anymore."

"If you don't level with me, I can't help."

"I don't know you."

"You do." She stopped in her tracks. "I'm Sky."

Clearly I'd offended her. "Knowing your name doesn't mean I know you."

"Except it does. Our names define us." She glanced up at the red moon.

"For Dryads?"

She nodded. "Yes."

"But I'm an outsider. I can't see the meaning the way you can."

"Roland didn't change you."

I glanced back at Owen again. And then at Adrian. No one was listening. "No. I was given a potion in the form of a paste."

"A paste?"

"Yeah… from a witch I met in New Orleans. I thought it was a joke, but well, it wasn't." I looked down at my body as though there was a physical manifestation of a change.

"Were you really with Violet and Hugh?"

"Yes. They were supposed to be helping me."

"Helping you with what?"

I debated. I'd already spilled lots of the beans. "To stop the change. They said seeking an audience with the Elders was the only chance I had."

"That's impossible," she hissed as we continued across the meadow. "If she said it was possible, she lied."

"I have to believe her. The other option is something I can't accept."

"The Elders aren't going to help. The Allure numbers are dwindling. Very few humans can accept the gift anymore."

"I don't want to accept it."

"You love him?" She looked at Owen.

I nodded. I loved him more than I believed possible, and it only got stronger each day.

"Always a complication." She waved her arm around.

"It's more than a complication."

"I don't know why Violet got your hopes up. There is nothing you can do."

"I refuse to believe that. There is always something." I clung to confidence I didn't know I had. I couldn't lose Owen after all this.

"I hope you keep this personality." She looked off into the distance.

"Keep it?"

"Yes. If you try really hard you can hold onto it."

"Changing takes away your personality?"

"Not at first, but as the years go on. It's the nature of things."

"How old are you?" I'd learned that someone's appearance said nothing about their true age.

"Older than I look. Although I'm not immortal. Only Allures and one other creature have that gift."

"You should call it a curse." A gift was supposed to be a good thing. I was curious about the other creature, but I didn't ask.

"Most gifts are also curses."

I sighed. "I wish I knew Violet's plan."

"Not to make things worse, but what if this was her plan?"

"What do you mean?"

"You know what I mean. What if the plan was to drop

125

you here? Bring you home, so to speak, while you wait things out."

"She wouldn't." I shook my head. I'd considered the same thing myself, but that didn't mean I was ready to admit it out loud.

"How well do you know Violet?" Sky glanced back at the others and then back at me.

"I know her." I didn't. Not really. She'd told me almost nothing about herself, and the only hint of her past I had was from Lonnie's story about an old ball. That wasn't much to go off.

"Violet is one of the oldest Allures I've ever met. She's not the type to come up with crazy schemes to help someone."

"She has a plan." The question was did the plan involve saving me from the Allure fate? I pushed away my doubts. The alternative was that I gave up everything. Violet had a plan to get the Elders to help me. I needed to figure out what it was so I could execute it myself.

"We'll be there soon," Adrian called up to us. Owen and Donna had fallen behind. I looked back and caught his eye. He gave me a slight smile.

I forced a smile back even though I didn't want to give one. I was feeling frustrated, terrified, and annoyed that he was talking to that Dryad so much. I'm not doing this for Owen I reminded myself. I'm doing this for me.

"Here we are." Sky gestured in front of her. "The Allure Village."

I looked around me. There were about a dozen small thatched roof cottages that were built into the hillside nestled between a forest and a river.

"This is the Allure village?"

"Were you expecting something different?"

"Something bigger." The Allures didn't seem like simple, hut dwelling people to me, and I definitely expected more than twelve houses. Did a lot of them live together?

"Your numbers are dwindling."

"You make it sound like that's a bad thing," I mumbled.

"Allures play an important role in the order of things," Adrian explained.

I turned to him hoping he'd continue.

"All creatures do, but the Allures are needed to keep the balance."

"The balance?" I asked. I wished something the Dryads said would make sense to me for once.

"You'll understand soon," Sky touched my arm.

"Which is Violet's house?" I looked over the homes.

"That one." Adrian pointed to the brown and green cottage at the top of the hill. "Roland's is over there." He pointed to one to the right of us.

"I want to see Violet's first."

"Hers before your maker's?" Adrian raised an eyebrow.

"I think she left something for me there." I grappled for a reasonable sounding excuse.

"And you are only telling us now?" Donna put a hand on her hip.

"I forgot. Just remembered." I hurried up the hill.

"Thanks for escorting us, but we'll be fine from here," Owen said from somewhere behind me. I assumed he'd follow, but either way we needed to start searching for any answers we could find.

"You'll come for the festival?" Donna called.

I glanced over my shoulder. Owen was right on my heels.

127

"We'll try." He caught up with me as I reached the door.

"Go on, try to open the door." Sky called up the hill.

"Wait. We need a key." Owen tried the door. It was locked.

"Daisy should be able to open it." Adrian called up. I heard footsteps behind us, and I knew one of the Dryads was following.

I put my hand on the doorknob. It warmed under my touch and gave way.

"You're an Allure," Donna said from behind us.

I nodded. I had it in me. That much was true.

I turned around and watched the three Dryads disappearing down the path.

Owen leaned in. "I know how to find them."

"What?"

"Shh." He put a finger to his lips.

"How?" I peered down the path. The Dryads were nowhere to be seen. "How do you know?"

"I can be persuasive."

"Meaning you flirted with the girl for info?" I didn't like that he flirted with her, but if it got us the information we needed, then I guessed it was well worth it.

"I didn't flirt, I gave her attention. She doesn't get much of it."

"Why not?" I found I actually cared. That was a good sign. Caring was feeling.

"Her family isn't all that important. I can relate."

"Says the advisor of the king…"

"I got my position out of my friendship with Levi, not my family."

I wanted to know more about Owen's family, but now

wasn't the time. "If we know, do we need to go inside at all?"

"It's probably a safer place for me to explain everything."

"Sky doesn't think Violet has a plan." I pushed open the door. I figured I should be forthcoming as well.

"Violet has one."

"How do you know?"

"Because her Allure doesn't work on me. She might have used it on Georgina and Mayanne but..."

"Wait, you're right. How didn't I think of that before? She might have been using her Allure on them."

"It wouldn't work on me or Levi, and neither woman sounded off to you, did they?"

I shook my head. "No, but either way, let's hope she did have some sort of plan."

twelve

owen

I turned on the one small lamp as we walked into the simple yet spacious home. From the outside it had appeared small, but the high ceilings and large hallways were nothing like what I expected. It was almost like an illusion. My eyes went immediately to the large window with a view of the entire valley below.

"We broke into someone's house." Daisy carefully closed the door behind us.

"If that was the case, would it have been so easy for you to open the front door?" The door hadn't budged when I touched it, but Daisy's touch worked immediately.

"It seems strange that any Allure can open it. Wouldn't that be a security or privacy issue? It can't be that simple."

"None of the Dryads were surprised, so it has to be pretty common."

"Or they want us to think that." Daisy walked into the living room. "We can't trust anyone anymore."

"You can trust me." I followed behind her. "But I agree with you about trusting anyone else. The Dryads seemed to know more than they were saying. I'm hoping this isn't some sort of trap."

"We can't know for sure, which is why we need to work fast."

"We can't go anywhere else tonight. We need to get food and sleep."

"You better not really be planning on going to that festival."

I smiled. "Really? Jealous of Donna?"

"This has nothing to do with jealousy, it has to do with fraternizing with the potential enemy."

"I know you aren't a fan, but I did get some information from her."

"You mentioned that earlier. Ready to share?"

"Yes." I put my hands on her hips. "But first I need something from you."

"What?" She scrunched up her forehead.

"This." I crushed my lips into hers. I'd been waiting hours to kiss her, and I wasn't going to give up the chance.

She wrapped her arms around my neck, pulling me closer. I lightly bit down on her lip. She moaned, and I intensified the kiss, soaking up her taste as I explored her mouth. I slipped my hand just underneath her t-shirt, wanting to feel her soft and warm skin.

She pushed my hand up higher, and I cupped her breast through her bra. She moaned as she ran her hand up and down my chest. Each touch set me on fire. I'd never get enough.

She bit down on my lip, and I groaned. I unclasped her

bra and cupped her breast without the fabric in the way. She moaned as I ran my fingers over her nipple.

I used my free hand to unbutton her pants, and I slipped my hand inside. She thrust her body against mine. I released her breast and pulled off her shirt, immediately discarding her bra.

I held her against me, reveling in the feel of her bare chest against mine. Everything about it was natural. We belonged together in a way that still made little sense. I'd never given much credence to fate, but I'd changed my mind. We were fated to be together. There was a higher power that wanted us together, and it made each day we spent together feel like a year in the intensity it created.

"I can feel your heartbeat," she whispered with her lips running down my neck.

"I can feel yours."

"I still can't believe you're here. Despite all this craziness, you're with me."

"I am." And I always would be.

"We can't do this though." She rested her head against my shoulder. "We can't let this go further."

"Because of how you feel, or because of everyone else?"

"Everyone else. The only feelings of mine I know are real right now are the ones I feel for you."

"Good. And although I don't want to stop, you're right." I let out a few deep breaths. My body was ready for her, but my mind knew that she was completely right.

I bent down and picked up her bra. Instead of handing it to her I put it on her myself. I moved around behind her to clasp it. Dressing her wasn't nearly as much fun as undressing her, but it was intimate in a different way.

She pulled on her shirt while I buttoned her jeans.

She ran her fingers through her hair that fell over her shoulder. "We'll finish that later."

I smiled. "Yes we will."

"What did Donna say?"

It took me a moment to answer. It was jarring to move from touching Daisy to discussing something serious. "The Glamour Realm is really several islands. We're on one of the largest ones. The Force is headquartered on one smaller one."

"And the Elders?"

"We have to travel to the farthest island in the chain in order to reach Energo. Once we get there we'll have to climb a massive mountain to get to Mount Majest." Not that I planned to climb anything. I'd fly us anywhere we needed to go.

"Fantastic." She pressed a hand to her forehead.

"There's more." I needed to share everything I knew. At least Donna had been chatty.

"Oh?"

"When they say we won't get an audience, they mean it. We won't even be allowed near the palace on our own." I wasn't used to being denied access anywhere. I'd grown up as the best friend of royalty, and I'd never had a door closed in my face. Now I had to learn to navigate a world where no one cared who or what I was.

"But we have to. There's no way to know how long Violet will be with the Force, or even if she's going to help." She paced around the worn wood floors of the main living space. The sparsely furnished place had a quirky yet homey feel.

"Which is why it's important we're here." I had to keep our confidence up. We needed to be ready for whatever came our way. "Maybe there's something here that can help."

"Maybe she left a clue. She specifically said she wanted us to see her home."

"Could be, but when would she have left it?"

"I don't know." She sighed. "It was only a thought. I'm also wondering about Taylor. When and how did she disappear? And what about Violet's past? What was the story behind the story Myrtle told us?"

I put my hands on her hips again and pulled her in. "You're cute when you're frustrated."

"I guess that means I'm cute a lot now."

I laughed. "You're breathtaking when you're happy." I knew I was moving us from the situation again, but I couldn't help it. Daisy was so stressed and sad. It was killing me.

"I'm happy when I'm with you."

"Are you?'" I looked deep into her eyes. I was constantly checking to make sure she was still there.

"Very." She leaned forward and brushed her lips against mine.

"I've missed you."

"Me too. And I got jealous. I'm ridiculous."

"Not ridiculous."

"I got jealous, and you were getting us information."

"I want you to be jealous." Being jealous meant she was still feeling. She needed to stay that way. Positive emotions were better, but negative ones could be strong.

"Oh yeah?"

I ran my lips down her neck. "It means you feel. You care."

She leaned her head to the side to give my lips better access. "No matter what happens, I'm going to remember your touch."

"I won't let you forget it. I won't let you forget anything."

"I love you."

I looked into her eyes again. "I love you too."

Tears streamed down her face. "I want to love you forever."

"And you will. I'll make sure of it." I wiped away the tears from her eyes.

"What are we looking for exactly?" She blinked a few times.

"Anything to tell us where we need to go."

"How do we do this? Are we really going to manually search her house?"

"Absolutely not!" a scratchy voice called from the dark corner of the room.

I transformed again, immediately on alert.

"Are the dramatics really that necessary?" The voice asked.

"Who are you?" Daisy's voice shook. We both watched the corner of the room where the voice came from.

"I'm Glendale." A small furry creature walked into the light.

"You're a cat. A cat who can talk?" I stared at the orange and white stripped animal.

"You're a man with wings. A man with wings that can talk?" he mocked.

"Have you been here the whole time?" Daisy asked.

"Concerned I witnessed your scene of intimacy?" He walked toward us. "Don't concern yourself with that, I've seen plenty, although much less over the past decades."

"Are you Violet's cat?" I couldn't really believe we were

engaging in conversation with a feline.

"I prefer to view our relationship as that of equals."

"But how does she view it?" Daisy put a hand on her hip.

"I don't know. I've never asked her. Maybe you should next time you see her."

"And when that will happen is the million dollar question."

"Where is she?" Glendale walked around us in the circle. "What are you doing here?"

"Isn't the bigger question who we are?" I still couldn't believe I was talking to a cat. At first I assumed he was a shifter, but most shifters couldn't talk in their animal form. Pterons are the exception since we stay partially human when we shift. I wondered if Glendale was something else entirely.

"I know who you are. Do you think I'd have been so hospitable if I didn't?"

"I don't know much about cats being hospitable." Daisy fidgeted uncomfortably as Glendale rubbed against her legs.

"Violet told me all about you." He moved over to my legs. I wanted to push him away, but he seemed talkative. "Both of you."

"Did she tell you what she was going to do to help me?" Daisy bent down to his level.

He bumped his head against hers. She startled and moved back. "No."

"And here I thought you could help."

"I can help." He purred.

"But you don't know anything." I held out a hand to Daisy and helped her up.

"I know *plenty*." The word plenty came out like a purr.

Daisy narrowed her eyes. "Then why is Violet in trouble with the Force?"

"Because of you."

"Because of me?" Daisy put her hand to her chest.

"Daisy has done nothing wrong."

"Except refuse the gift." Glendale rubbed against Daisy's legs again. "But I said she was in trouble because of Daisy, not that Daisy caused it."

"Meaning?"

"Meaning she's in trouble for aiding you when her superior told her not to."

"Louie." His name slipped off my tongue with distaste.

"Exactly."

"What are they going to do to her? And Hugh?"

"They have Hugh too?" Glendale twitched his tail.

"Yes."

"Wonderful." He purred loud and deep.

"Wonderful?"

"That man needs to be put in his place."

"Please answer me. What are they going to do with her?"

"They'll let her go with a warning. No one really wants to mess with Violet. It's too dangerous. She's stronger than half the Force."

"Then why did she let them take her in?"

"Because it's the rules."

"Do you know how to find the Force? The island it's on?"

"Yes, we will leave tomorrow first thing."

"You're coming?"

"I need to see that Violet is released immediately."

"But not tonight?"

"No. Not on the first night of the blood moon festival."

"Scared of the Dryads?" I raised an eyebrow. Unless these Dryads were completely different than the ones back home, the cat had nothing to worry about. They loved nature and animals no matter what form.

"It's not the Dryads I'm afraid of." His eyes narrowed down into small slits.

"Then who is it?"

"I want you to sleep tonight. You'll be safer if you stay indoors." He circled Daisy's legs.

"The Dryads invited us to the festival."

"Sure they did. I'm not surprised at all."

"So they were knowingly luring us to danger?"

"The festival itself is safe, but traveling to and from isn't."

"But I thought Allures were super powerful. Who would hurt me?" Daisy sounded more confident than usual.

"You are still partly human. I can tell."

"What if you're the one trapping us?" I asked. "You want us to stay here."

"You were already planning on staying. I heard the two of you."

"I've changed my mind." I wasn't getting tricked again, especially not by a cat.

"I'm not going out there tonight." Glendale turned his back and raised his tail.

"Not even to get to Violet sooner?" Daisy made her voice low and sweet.

"Violet will be fine another night. Me, on the other hand, do you think I'm good at defending myself?"

"Cats are really clever, and don't you have claws and sharp teeth?"

"I appreciate you making me sound like a lion, but I'm

small in size."

I heard footsteps. "Where you expecting someone else?" I asked the cat.

The fur on the back of Glendale stuck up. "No, this is trouble. Hide Daisy. They came for her."

"Where?" Daisy asked quietly. "Where can we hide?"

The front door swung open, and I instinctively jumped in front of Daisy. Glendale arched his back.

A man dressed in a black suit with a matching black tie strode into the room. "Well, well, well. This was easy."

"What are you doing here?" I glared at the intruder. He was even taller and larger than me. Since he'd opened the door on his own without the sound of a key, I assumed he was an Allure.

"I'm collecting my bounty. It was much easier than expected."

"What bounty?" I didn't know what he was talking about, but I knew it couldn't be good.

"For the new Allure. It was twice the usual bounty reward. The Force must really want her."

"The Force?" I struggled to stay in control. I needed a plan. I couldn't let him take Daisy, but I had no idea how many others were waiting outside.

"Yes. I see you've heard of our esteemed body of law enforcement."

"Maybe."

"Daisy? Come out little one."

I held a hand behind me to keep her back. There was no reason for her to engage with this guy. I glanced around the room. I didn't see anywhere to hide her if a fight broke out. Hopefully she'd stay low.

"You've been a bad girl, and you're leaving Violet and Hugh to pay for it all alone." He snickered.

Daisy made a low noise behind me.

"You can make this easy or hard."

"We're not going with you." Daisy stepped to my side.

"Of course you are. The question is whether you come easily, or whether you get yourself hurt in the process. Either way, you are coming with us."

"Us? I only see you."

"Oh yeah?" He smiled. "Come in, Barton."

Another man, dressed in a similar manner as the first one walked in carrying a small cane.

I smiled to myself. I could take two Allures easily, with or without a cane. The trick was keeping Daisy out of the way so she didn't get hurt. "We're not going with you."

"I don't really care whether you come. The bounty is on the girl, not you."

"She isn't going anywhere without me." I gritted my teeth.

"Then come join the fun." His lips twisted into an evil smile.

I shook my head. "No."

"Have it your way." He gestured for Barton to turn off the light.

As soon as the light switched off my eyes quickly adjusted to the darkness. Suddenly a hazy black shadow appeared in front of me. I stepped away, but then the shadowy haze appeared to multiply, until a half dozen surrounded me. I was separated from Daisy.

I punched one, but my arm went through it as though it were a vapor. I tried to step outside of it, but I couldn't. I was completely engulfed by the darkness. All of the black vapors coalesced together around me, creating a single form that nearly suffocated me.

"Owen!" Daisy screamed from behind me. I turned to watch the first intruder throw her over his shoulder.

I fought harder against the dark vapor, but I couldn't move. I was stuck in the dark presence. The harder I fought, the more labored my breathing became until I felt suffocated.

"Have fun with the Shadow," He called before he walked to the door.

"Daisy!" I screamed in vain as she was pulled from the house. Out of the corner of my eye I noticed Glendale slip outside. I hoped he was really on our side and stronger than he claimed to be.

thirteen

daisy

I struggled against the man holding me. He was an Allure, I could feel it, but he seemed even stronger as I kicked his chest as hard as I could.

"Stop fighting me." He pressed down on my legs so I couldn't kick anymore.

"No." I punched his back. "I will not stop fighting until you let me go and bring me back to my friend."

"Your friend?" His voice was hoarse and low. "Something tells me he's more than a friend."

"What the hell do you care?"

"Because that's what is causing all the problems."

"Last time I checked I wasn't causing any problems. Other people were causing the problems." I wriggled against him again, but all that got me was a tighter grip.

"Violet and Hugh are in a heap of trouble because of you. You've been given a gift, quit fighting it."

"You're an Allure?"

"No kidding, cupcake." He pulled me along across a dense forest. Wasn't there anyone around to see? I was in trouble, but that didn't mean I wasn't worried about Owen.

"That's why you're such a jerk."

"Oh yeah?" He roughly adjusted me in his arms. "Hating your own now?"

"Not my own. I don't want to be one." I gritted my teeth. I was angry, and there was no one around to calm me down. Maybe that was a good thing.

"Not wanting something doesn't change it."

"It should."

"You sound like a spoiled brat." He tightened his grip.

"You're hurting me," I grunted.

"No I'm not."

"How would you—"

He laughed. "Can't fool an Allure, sweetie."

"Could you stop with the pet names?"

"Don't like them?"

"No. Not at all." I kept him talking to keep myself sane. Silence wasn't going to be a good thing.

"What would you rather me call you?"

"Nothing." I tried again to loosen his grip. It resulted in him holding me even tighter.

"I have to call you something. You won't care what I call you in a few days anyway."

"A few days?" My chest clenched. "That's all the time I have left?"

"You make it sound like you're dying."

"I am. Losing my ability to feel is death." I stopped struggling. If he tightened his hold again I wouldn't be able to breath.

143

"Quit it. Stop feeling sorry for yourself."

"Why?" I ground my teeth. "I'm about to lose everything I've ever loved and makes me who I am."

"You're going to live forever. You're going to be one of the most powerful creatures any world has ever seen. You should feel lucky."

"There's nothing lucky about my life." That wasn't entirely true. I was lucky to be born to a loving family and to have found Owen. Having his love was lucky, but then there was everything else. The magic, the vampires, becoming an Allure. They were the antithesis of luck.

"Stop." He spun me around. "It's time for you to face the music."

I shook my head. It was the only resistance I could give. "I know you can't feel, but I can. I'm going to enjoy the last days I have. Please. Let me see Owen."

"Why? What's the point?"

"I love him."

"And that matters? Spending more time with him will only make it harder on him. It's been a long time since I've loved anyone, but I wouldn't think that's how you'd want to treat him. Is it?" He sounded like Violet. Maybe that's how all Allures viewed love, but I wasn't an Allure yet. I knew that Owen would want the time together even if it made the future harder. He'd have to move on either way.

"So wanting to see him makes me selfish? Is that what you're trying to say?"

"Not exactly."

"Just say it then? What's your point?" I blinked, attempting to hold back tears that were threatening to spill. I refused to cry in front of this guy.

"You need to focus on the big picture. You are in trouble. Serious trouble."

"I know I am. I'm losing myself." In the end that was more important than anything the Force could do to me.

"Stop worrying about losing your human side. It's already gone."

"Just tell me. Where is he? Is he still at Violet's house?" I hoped somewhere in this man was some shred of human understanding. Violet had it. Maybe he did too.

"He's being escorted back home as we speak."

I shook my head out of disbelief this time. Owen couldn't leave. Not yet. "No. That's not possible."

"Not possible?" He pulled me forward into his chest. "Do you really think you are in a position to argue about what's possible?"

"I have nothing left to lose." I didn't have anything left if I couldn't stop the change, and I wasn't going to be able to stop it on my own. I had to escape this jerk, find Mount Majest, and beg an audience with the Elders. Nothing about that would be easy, especially without someone to help.

"Actually you have plenty more to lose."

"Is that a threat?" I shivered. Was he talking about Owen? My family? Nothing else mattered. I was done worrying about protecting myself.

"No, it's reality."

"How much further do we have to go?" I wanted to know how much longer I had to escape. I assumed it would be easier to escape out in the woods rather than with the Force.

"Tired already?" He sneered.

"No, but—" I noticed movement out of the corner of my eye. "If it's far we should probably keep moving."

"You're suddenly in a rush now?" He asked suspiciously. "Do you think making me paranoid is going to change anything?"

I shook my head. "No. At least if he get to the Force I can see Violet."

"That's the first logical thing you've said since I met you."

"Yeah, well." I needed to play it cool. Whatever was out there didn't want to be seen by my captor. I took that as a good sign.

He turned me around in his arms and continued his march forward.

"You never answered my question."

"Which one?" His hold was lighter now at least.

"How far are we? I'm tired. There I admitted it."

"You're weak. You really need to let go of that human side."

"It sounds like I don't have a choice about it."

"You don't. I'm only pointing out why losing it will be a good thing."

"Sure." I noticed the movement again out of the corner of my eye, but I played it cool. "Could you loosen your hold?"

"No."

"I won't run away."

"And why would I trust you?"

"Where else do I have to go?"

"Back to find lover boy." He did a high pitched impersonation of a female.

I ignored his failed impression. "I don't know how to get home."

"I'm not letting go of you until we reach the Force. I'll be in a lot of trouble if I lose you. I'll also be out of a lot of money."

"Can we at least stop for some water? I'm thirsty."

"Once again, you need to let go of that human side."

"Gotcha. No need to keep repeating yourself."

"There's a river with fresh drinkable water nearby." He turned deeper into the forest.

"Why are you doing this job?"

"I already told you, it's double the usual bounty."

"And you are that hard up for money?"

He laughed. "Money? I'm an Allure. You think I can't get enough money on my own?"

"Then what's the bounty?"

"You really don't know anything yet."

"No, I don't. No one tells me anything."

"It's no wonder Violet hasn't told you."

"Why not?" I froze. I knew I wasn't going to like what he had to tell me.

"I don't want to make you angrier than I have already."

"Tell me."

"You really want to know?" He turned me so I was looking at him again.

"Yes. I want to know."

"What do you think it is? What do you think an Allure would want that they can't get themselves?"

I thought about it. Allures could have nearly everything. Except for one thing. "Feelings."

"You are smart."

"The bounty is for feelings? They pay you with feelings?"

"Not exactly. It's for a glimpse of a memory with feeling."

"One memory? And just a glimpse?"

He looked me straight in the eye. "After years without

feeling you will understand how strong a glimpse can be."

"You said this was double the bounty. What does that mean?"

"I get to choose two memories, or one twice."

"Which will you choose?" It didn't matter that we were talking about turning me in to get it. I had to know. Rational or not, I wanted to understand this man.

"One memory twice."

"What's it a memory of?"

"My parents on the day I graduated high school."

"Oh." I reflected back on my own high school graduation.

"They were proud of me. Beaming. I miss that feeling. Of knowing I made someone proud." He sounded far off.

I blinked back tears as I thought of how my mother had cried. It had rained halfway through, but we didn't care we were wet. High school was over, and the rest of our life was still in front of us.

He broke me from my thoughts. "And that's exactly what Violet wanted from you. Maybe she wanted to take you straight to the Elders so she could get a bigger reward. Cut out the middle man of the Force."

I shook my head. "No. She wouldn't use me that way."

"Why not? You have so much to learn."

"Because she wouldn't." I had less confidence. Why wouldn't Violet turn me in for access to memories with emotion? It was the only thing she couldn't get herself.

"Keep telling yourself whatever you want. We're getting water, and we're moving on. I have a bounty to collect."

"Yes, your bounty." I was overcome by a sadness like none I'd ever had. I was going to become one of them. A being willing to do everything for even a glimpse of emotion. What was the point of going on?

fourteen

owen

Feeling helpless was becoming far too common for me. I was supposed to be invincible. The strongest of the strong, yet once again I found myself unable to protect the girl I loved. The darkness was relentless, but if I stayed completely still, I could get some air. Whatever this blackness was, I'd never come across it before. The first Allure had called it a Shadow, and that was a good name. It had only appeared when the light was turned off, which meant I had to find a way to get the lights turned on if I wanted to get rid of it. At least in theory. Since I couldn't move, getting to the lamp was going to be difficult.

Barton broke his silence. "Why did you come here? Why not stay home where it's safe?"

I struggled to speak, but no words came out.

Barton sighed. "You can let him breath."

The smothering lessened, and I tried again to speak. It wasn't easy, but after a few deep breaths I muttered a few words, "I came here with Daisy."

"Forget about Daisy. She isn't going to care about you in a few days. I can see the change. She'll be full Allure soon and won't even give you the time of day."

"Not if I can help it," I grunted. It hurt to speak from inside the Shadow as it continued to restrain my movements, but it felt good to at least breathe.

"You can't help it. There is absolutely nothing you can do."

"Yes, there is." There was always a chance.

"Why are you so full of false optimism? It's going to get you nowhere."

"Why do you care?" I choked out. "Why bother to keep me here? Let me go so I can fail and prove you right."

"The only place you are going is back to your own realm. You don't belong here."

"Yes, you've said that before." I didn't belong there. Neither did Daisy.

"I'm waiting for back up, and then we're out of here."

"Backup? If I'm so weak and helpless, can't you do it yourself?" Taunting your captor wasn't always a good idea, but maybe if I distracted him the Shadow would lay off. Somehow he was controlling it.

"Of course I could."

"Then what are you waiting for?"

"I'm following protocol." Barton restlessly strode back and forth in front of the door twirling his cane.

"I wasn't aware Allures had protocol."

"We're as organized as you are."

"Glad you think The Society is organized."

"Shut up. The time will go faster if you keep your mouth

closed." He peered out the window.

Suddenly the door burst open, and Violet immediately turned on the light. The tightening around me stopped abruptly, and I could breathe normally. The dark forms were gone.

"Hello, Barton. Still playing with your toys?" Violet strode toward the startled Allure and grinned.

I shook my arm. I could move. I took several deep breaths, trying to get myself back to normal. Violet and Barton were my best clues to finding Daisy.

"You're supposed to be with the Force." Barton stepped back from the door. "I'm only in your house because Gabriel said I should."

"Then you can leave my house now." She pointed to the doorway.

"Fine, I need to deport this one anyway."

"He can stay. He's in my house after all." She shot me a warning glance, and I took it to mean I needed to stay quiet.

"Gabriel's orders were to take him home."

"And I say he stays." She walked over and stopped mere inches from him. "Are you really going to refuse to listen to me?"

"No." He shook his head. "I'm leaving."

"Good, but first tell me, where is Gabriel? I fear he has my good friend with him."

"He's taking her to the Force."

"Thank you, you can go." She shooed him to the door.

"That was far too easy." My breathing had finally returned to its normal state.

"Getting rid of him?" She closed the door behind him.

"Yes."

"I can be rather persuasive when I want to be." She ran her hand over a few dusty books on the bookshelf.

"We have no time to waste. They have Daisy."

"I understand that." She smiled. "Didn't you hear me asking Barton about it?"

"Then why are you still standing here? We need to go."

"We will. I'm deciding on the best course of action."

"The best course of action is to leave and rescue her."

"Except that we are likely outnumbered."

"I can take them." Anger and frustration pulsed through my body. I could feel adrenaline building up.

"Like you took them just now?" She raised an eyebrow. "I'm not looking to destroy your masculine confidence, but you can't take them. You don't understand what you are up against, and you underestimated your opponent."

"I won't next time. I'll know."

"You'll be distracted. You're always going to be distracted where Daisy is concerned."

I had so many questions for Violet, but they could wait. We had to find Daisy. "Then what do you suggest?"

"Have you seen a cat?"

"Glendale?" Was she really worrying about her cat at a time like this?

"Yes. He introduced himself, I see." Her eyes twinkled.

"I have quite a few questions about your feline friend, but right now my concern is finding Daisy."

"Do you know where the cat is?"

I sighed. "He left when they took Daisy. Maybe he couldn't find his litter box."

She rolled her eyes. "Or he was following them. That's great news. He won't let them get all the way to the Force."

"The cat is going to stop them?" I raised an eyebrow. Clearly the cat was more than the usual household variety pet. Maybe the ability to speak wasn't his only skill.

"Yes. He has plenty of tricks up his sleeves."

"Even if he has no sleeves…" I hoped she had a better plan than simply relying on the cat.

She shook her head at my weak attempt at a joke. "Let's find our girl."

"Our girl?"

She lifted her chin. "Yes. I want to help Daisy too."

"Even though you can't feel. I'm never going to understand that." And I was always going to question her motives.

"It shouldn't matter. We both want to get her back." She hurried out the door, and I didn't see any alternative but to follow.

It was still dark, but I could see the barest hint of the sunrise. I wasn't sure if the morning was going to bring any relief from our situation. All I could think about was finding Daisy.

"Why does the Force want her?" I still didn't understand what was going on. "And why did they take you and Hugh?"

"Louie. He turned us in. All new Allures must be checked in with the Force."

"Then why didn't they take Daisy right off?"

"She isn't full Allure, so they couldn't grab her when she transported."

"They can grab Allures when you transport? Isn't that a little extreme?"

"Or convenient for them, depending on how you look at it."

"Or incredibly annoying."

"Yes, that's another way to look at it." She smiled at me over her shoulder.

I followed Violet out of the Allure village. We walked across a large clearing and toward the jungle again. Neither of us said anything as we moved at a fast pace. I didn't know the landscape, so I put my trust in Violet. No matter what her intentions were, she seemed intent on finding Daisy. That meant, if only temporarily, our goals were united.

"I'm not trying to double cross you." She broke the silence.

"I never said you were." I only thought it.

"Not with words, but your eyes and body language say it all. You don't trust me."

"Can you blame me?" She'd started the conversation, so I went with it. "You brought us to a new realm and disappeared. Did you think we'd be happy about that?"

"That wasn't by choice."

"Oh yes, because you were picked up by the Force." I was tired of excuses and the runaround.

"I assure you that wasn't our plan."

"Then what was?" I pushed through some long and tangled vines.

"To get Daisy to Mount Majest. You know that. Seeing the Force wasn't part of the plan, but they are one of the inconveniences we have to deal with."

"Then why did we come this way? Wasn't it supposed to be easier than going straight to Energo?" So far it was anything but easy.

"There's complications with cutting through other nations, but we won't get noticed this way."

"Whatever you say." I continued to trample through the jungle. I saw no sign of Daisy, and I sincerely hoped this wasn't a trap. "Is this to avoid being seen too?"

"It's a short cut. I know which way Gabriel is going."

"Sure. Speaking of where people are going, where's Hugh?" I didn't miss the guy, but his absence didn't go unnoticed.

"He's procuring us transportation."

"So you didn't leave him behind?"

"No." She smiled. "I'm sure you would have been disappointed if I had."

"He doesn't bother me as much as Roland."

"I wonder why?" She laughed.

"At least Hugh knows his appropriate boundaries."

"I find it interesting that you haven't asked what kind of transportation he's getting."

"I'd assume he's getting a boat."

"Yes. You understand we're on an island?"

"Yes, the whole water surrounding us thing made it obvious."

"You haven't seen more than one shore." She gave me an annoyed look over her shoulder.

"True, but I figured it out, and we need to get to another island so a boat sounds reasonable. If you want to fly I have my own wings for that." I'd never grown to like planes. I always felt stifled.

"Fine, you're right. We don't have much time before we need to meet him."

"We need as much time as it takes to get Daisy. There's no point meeting him without her."

"It's going to be easier since you have wings." She turned,

and we moved into a less lush area of the jungle.

Now that was a plan I could get behind. "My wings are part of your plan?"

"Yes. Gabriel won't be expecting an air attack since he will assume the shadow still has you."

"Good point." I bent down and ran my hands over new footprints in the dirt. "We caught their trail."

"And you're a tracker too." She grinned.

"I have many skills."

"Lucky Daisy."

I ignored the sexual innuendo in her statement. "Let's go."

I took the lead, following the footprints. They veered north before zagging off in a strange direction. The trail wasn't leading to any shore.

"Water." Violet explained. "He's taking her to the stream."

"He's concerned with getting her drinking water?" Somehow I doubted that.

"Probably. Daisy can be mighty persuasive."

"To humans and some paranormals, not to Allures."

Violet shrugged. "You don't know that for sure."

I sped up my pace. Knowing we were getting closer gave me new motivation.

We were almost there. I could hear the flowing water. I released my wings and flew up to a tall tree. I didn't wait to confer with Violet. We were close, and I wasn't losing my chance.

I flew quietly and scoured the landscape. Daisy was seated on a rock by the water. The Allure held her arm in a tight grip. I noticed Glendale hiding in the brush nearby.

"I'll be ready in a minute." She looked up. She caught my

eye and smiled for a split second before composing herself. She didn't seem surprised to see me, and my heart soared. She'd known I'd find her eventually. Of course she didn't realize Violet had saved me.

"What? What did you see?" Gabriel looked up. I quickly moved lower behind a tree so I was out of his view.

"Nothing," she hurriedly replied. "I was just looking."

"You saw something." Gabriel grabbed her and yanked her off the rock.

Watching him handle her roughly was more than I could handle. I didn't pause to think. I swooped down and pulled her from his hold as I knocked him to the ground.

I flew back up to the tree so I could assess her. "Are you hurt?" We didn't have much time, but I had to make sure she didn't need medical attention.

"No." She rested her head on my chest. "Are you?"

"I'm okay." Other than a damaged ego, I was fine.

"What do we do about him?" She pointed down to where Gabriel was now talking to Violet and Glendale. She looked between the figures on the ground and me. "Violet? You found her?"

"Actually she found me." I wasn't eager to relay how I'd had to be saved by an Allure.

I listened to the argument below. Violet wagged a finger in Gabriel's face. "How dare you. After all these years, you turned on me?"

"It was a double bounty, Vi. What did you expect? You want the same thing."

She shook her head. "I want to help the girl. Stay out of my way."

"Not this time. I need this." His eyes bore into hers. "I

157

need *it*."

"I'm sorry, but you're going to have to find another way."

"No, you are."

"You think you're going to stop me?" Violet put a hand on her hip.

"Yes."

Glendale made a loud hiss, and the ground started to tremble. Within moments at least a dozen striped tigers moved out from deep in the jungle. The largest approached Gabriel and roared loud enough to shake the trees as the other tigers circled around.

Gabriel groaned. "Really? Cats? Is that really your plan?"

"Think you can fly one more?" Violet called up to me.

"Yes."

"And a cat?" Glendale flicked his tail from side to side.

"Yes." I would do whatever it took. We had Daisy back, and as much as I didn't want to admit it, I had Violet to thank for that.

"Violet, no. You can't leave me here." Gabriel gazed at the tigers surrounding him.

"You're clever. You'll find a way out. Besides, they don't like Allures. They won't eat you."

I swooped back down and picked up Violet and the cat. Flying two people was new, as was flying a cat. I wouldn't mention that part to the guys.

"Glendale?" Daisy asked as I flew.

"Yes?"

"If you could summon giant cats, why didn't you do that when they first arrived?"

"I cannot summon them out of thin air. They live in this jungle."

"Do they talk, like you?" Daisy asked.

"No."

"Fly to the north shore," Violet directed.

I tuned everyone out and focused on flying toward the shore.

fifteen

daisy

Every few hours I reevaluated the term crazy. As soon I was accepting one situation I was hit with another. They changed so fast it was making me dizzy, but none of that mattered as Owen flew us away from the river. I was back with Owen, and somehow everything was going to be okay.

He flew for miles, and I forced myself to keep my questions to myself. Owen was using all of his energy to fly us, and I wasn't about to make things harder on him by flustering Violet or anything. Instead I focused on how lucky I was to get to spend a few more minutes with Owen. Selfish or not, I savored his touch and the feel of his body against mine.

I closed my eyes, inhaling his scent and every single sensation. I wasn't ready to give up, but even if I failed, I wouldn't forget. I'd find a way to feel the love again. Not only for Owen, but for my family also.

Finally he slowed and landed on the sandy beach. The

beach was empty aside from a few sea birds walking along the water's edge.

Owen walked off a few feet, and I assumed it was because he didn't want us to see how tired he was. I still couldn't believe he'd carried Violet, me, and a cat so far. His wings were strong, but that had to have been pushing it.

I gave him space and instead gazed out at the water. I noticed a large yacht in the distance.

"That must be Hugh." Violet waved even though I assumed Hugh was too far away to see.

I'd barely talked to her yet, and I wasn't sure what to say. Did I confront her about her motivation to glimpse memories with emotion and watch her response? It all had to tie back to that New Orleans ball. It had to. The logical side of me kept my mouth shut. Aside from seeing the Elders, I had no plan. If I confronted her she might not take me to them. Whether she was turning me in or not, I still needed to get there. I could figure out what to do next once we arrived.

"I missed you." Owen's arms slid around my waist, and I leaned back into him.

"I missed you too."

"Does that mean you won't run off on me again?" he teased.

His teasing was exactly what I needed. Things were so crazy that I needed to find some normalcy anywhere I could.

"I'll try not to, but did you see that Allure?" I teased him right back.

"Did my heroic acts make you forget him?"

"Yes." I turned in his arms. "Thank you. I'm starting to lose count of how many times you've saved me."

"Doesn't matter. As I always tell you, I'd do it anytime."

I watched as the boat pulled near the shore. "Our ride is here."

He leaned in. "Trust no one."

"I was going to tell you the same thing," I whispered back.

"We need to get to Mount Majest either way."

"Once again, I was going to say the same thing." We were definitely on the same page.

"Finally get free, bird?" Hugh called from the deck of the boat.

"Hugh?" I spun around and looked up at him.

"It's me in the flesh. Miss me?" He smirked.

"Not really, but thanks for getting the boat." I looked at the nearly forty-foot wooden yacht.

"No problem. Glad I could be of service, but I'm waiting for your usual question."

It took me a moment to follow his train of thought. "I was hoping you didn't have to steal vehicles here."

"Not steal, borrow."

"Great." Even in the Glamour Realm I couldn't avoid feeling like a criminal.

"Come aboard," he called. "I promise you're going to like it."

"It doesn't really matter whether I like it or not. We need the ride."

"Testy, testy." He grinned. "Need help getting on?"

"That won't be necessary." Owen wrapped his arms around me and flew us over onto the deck.

"Showing off?" Hugh rested his hand on the wheel.

"More like saving Daisy the energy. She's had a busy few days."

"So have you." He smirked. "So tell me, did you get out on your own, or did Violet save you?" He spun the wheel and pushed the throttle forward. The engine roared to life.

Owen shrugged. "Violet helped."

Hugh nodded. "I'm impressed you'll admit it."

"Why wouldn't I?" Owen kept his arms around me. "I have nothing to prove."

"Or so you say."

"Speaking of helping, want to help me?" Violet called up.

"Go ahead." I touched Owen's arm. The sooner Violet got on, the sooner we could go.

Owen flew down and picked her up. He landed next to us.

Violet grinned. "Everyone ready to head to Energo?" She was annoyingly cheerful again, as if my entire fate wasn't hanging in the balance.

"How long is this trip going to take?" Owen led me over to the railing of the ship.

"A few hours." Violet tied her hair up into a ponytail. She managed to make it look perfect despite not having a brush or comb. I wondered if becoming an Allure would suddenly make my hair perfect. I pushed away the thought. It didn't matter. It wasn't going to happen. We were going to stop the change in time. "You two can sleep first if you want."

"Sleep? This trip is going to take long enough that we sleep in shifts?" I'd thought she said it was only a few hours.

"Not in shifts, but enough time for you to get some rest."

I looked over at Owen. We needed some alone time. "I wouldn't mind it."

"I agree Daisy needs rest, but why do you want her to have it?" Owen studied Violet. "How do we know you are really taking us to Energo?"

"Either trust us and get some alone time or don't." Hugh shrugged. "What's it going to be?"

"We need alone time." I tugged on Owen's arm. Stupid or not, I wasn't wasting another minute of the time we had left.

sixteen

owen

The bedroom in the hull of the boat was small but luxurious. I locked the door behind us, even though Violet or Hugh walking in was the least of my worries.

Daisy sighed and walked further into the room before stopping right in front of the double bed.

"Promise you're okay?" I ran my eyes up and down her body in search of any evidence of physical injury. I'd found one already. Her wrist was red from where Gabriel had gripped her too tight. He'd pay for it eventually, but at the moment I was just so relieved Daisy was okay.

"I'm fine." She ran her hand up my arm.

"I'm sorry." I finally said the words that had been spinning through my head since landing on the boat. Now that we'd found Daisy and the adrenaline had worn off, I was reminded of what happened at Violet's house.

"For?" She lifted her head up.

I chose my words carefully. I didn't want to sound like I

was feeling sorry for myself, but I wanted her to understand I was going to make sure it never happened again. "Allowing my weakness to put you in danger." I shouldn't have been so confident. I'd had no idea what I was up against.

"It's my weakness that has us in this positon to begin with."

"Not your weakness. Your strength." The fact that Daisy was able to handle the Allure essence was a testament to her strength. As was her ability to fight it from changing her completely.

"What do you mean?" She sat down on the edge of the bed.

I sat down next to her. "If you were weak you wouldn't have taken to the Allure essence. It was your strength it was attracted to."

"But then my strength became my weakness."

"This conversation is getting too complicated." I rubbed her back gently.

"Then stop talking about being weak. You saved me, focus on that."

"I shouldn't have let him take you to begin with."

"You had no choice. That thing had you." She put a hand on my leg.

"I had no idea that Shadows even existed. It's a crazy species." I'd never seen anything like it. I would tell Levi all about it as soon as I saw him. The Shadows could be a real threat to The Society. We needed to develop a defense against them.

"Isn't it hard to believe all this exists," she spread out her arms, "and no one in our world even knows it?"

"I guess it's similar to how most humans don't know that

paranormal creatures exist either." Even Daisy didn't know about us a few years before.

"When this is over I want to go away somewhere where we can forget about everything but humans and Pterons." She smiled.

I pulled her close. "We can go anywhere and everywhere you want." I would go anywhere she wanted. I'd never been much of a traveler, but with Daisy any place would be exciting.

"Do you like the beach?"

"The beach?" I thought about the beach we'd just been on. I probably would have found it beautiful under different circumstances.

"Yeah. We've never talked about stuff like that."

"We do have a lot more to talk about." Tons. There was so much more I needed to learn about her, and I couldn't wait to have the chance.

"Is it strange?"

"Is what strange?" I ran my hands through her hair.

"How strong our feelings are for each other considering how little we know of one another?"

"No, because that's not how love works. It's not about the details, it's the big picture and the feeling."

"Have you ever been in love? Before now?" She crawled onto my lap straddling me.

I rested my hands on her hips. "I thought I was once, but I wasn't."

"How did you figure out you were wrong?" She shifted on my lap, moving her chest even closer to mine.

"When it ended. She hurt me, there was no question about that, but it wasn't because I loved her. What about you?

Have you been in love?"

"Before you?" She shook her head. "Never."

"Good." I smiled.

"Glad to be my first love?"

"Glad to be your first, your last, and your only." I brushed my lips against hers.

"That line has several meanings, you know."

"Everlasting."

"That's better." She ran her hand up and down my bare chest. I wasn't sure where I was going to find another shirt, but at the moment I didn't care.

"I agree." I left tiny kisses up and down her neck.

She moaned, and it urged me on.

"I know we're going to fix this, but I don't want to waste a minute." She moved back and pulled off her t-shirt.

"We should never waste a minute." I reached around and unclasped her bra. I tossed the bra and immediately claimed her breasts with my hand and my mouth. She rewarded me with a moan and she wriggled on my lap.

She unbuttoned my pants and took me in her hand. I groaned, and bit down lightly on her nipple.

"I need you," she breathed against my neck.

"No rushing this." I unbuttoned her jeans.

She moved off my lap and slid her jeans off.

Before she could follow with her panties, I took care of them myself as I stepped out of my own pants and boxers.

"I could stare at your naked body for hours." My eyes moved over every inch of her.

"You could do a lot more than stare."

"Oh yeah?" I closed the space between us, returning my mouth to her breast as my hand slid down between our bodies.

"I will never get enough of your touch."

"That's a good thing, because you're always going to get it." I moved my hand between her legs, slipping one finger inside of her.

She moaned and took me in her hand again. Her touch was strong yet gentle, and I couldn't get enough of it.

She thrust her body against mine, and I slid in another finger.

She gasped. We were both struggling to stay standing, but neither of us were eager to change that yet.

"Owen," She moaned my name, and I couldn't take it anymore. I lifted her up and laid her down on the bed.

I moved beside her and left kisses up and down her entire body while she watched me with wide eyes. "I am going to worship every inch of you."

Her eyes met mine. "It's all yours."

"Forever?"

"Forever." She reached up and pulled my head down to hers. Her lips crushed into mine, and I responded immediately. I needed more of her taste.

I moved over her while continuing the kiss. My tongue tangled with hers as I thrust inside of her, returning to my favorite place. She opened up to me, as I continued to move in and out until my entire length was inside.

She raked her nails down my back, and I continued to kiss her, loving the combination of being inside her body and mouth. She moaned against my mouth, urging me on. I sped things up, making it harder and faster. She wrapped her legs around me, and I pulled her closer.

"Owen," She moaned. She was getting close, but close

wasn't good enough. Her breathing picked up and she panted. "Owen."

I held myself back until she was going over the edge, and then I shuddered as I reached my own release. I relaxed, remaining inside of her.

"Don't move," she ordered.

I kissed her lips gently. "If it were up to me I never would."

"I love the feeling of you pulsing inside of me."

"That makes two of us."

She bit down on my lip, and I groaned before returning the gesture.

"And I still want you."

"Now?"

She nodded.

I moved my mouth to her breast. I'd never done foreplay while still inside a girl post sex. It was such a crazy backwards thing, but it worked. Too well. I was hard again within moments.

She grinned. "Now that's a great sensation."

I laughed. "Was that your plan all along?"

"Maybe," she smiled coyly.

"Well, it worked." I ran my lips down her neck while I prepared to start all over again.

seventeen

daisy

"We're crazy."

"Why would you say that?"

"We're on a boat going who knows where, driven by Allures who may or may not be on our side, yet we're down here naked." I ran my hand down his bare chest to emphasize my point, and because he was too irresistible not to touch.

"Yes, we are naked, aren't we?" He pulled me on top of him.

I giggled. He was the only man to ever make me giggle. "That wasn't a cue that we should have more sex, Owen."

"Then what was it a cue for?" He kissed my neck. He was acting so different. So relaxed. Maybe sex had an effect on him too.

"Unfortunately, it was a cue to get dressed."

"Very unfortunate." His lips moved further down my neck, and I knew I had to put on the breaks.

I rolled off of him. "It's time to get dressed."

"I suppose it's the responsible thing to do." He pulled me to his side.

"It's the only thing." I reluctantly detangled myself from his arms.

"After we stop the change, we're spending an entire day in bed."

"What about food?"

"You've never cooked naked?" He handed me my clothes from the floor.

"No." I stepped into my underwear and clasped my bra. "Can't say I have."

He sighed. "And I lose my favorite view."

I raised an eyebrow. "Your favorite view?"

"Yes. Is there a problem with that?"

"There are plenty of other better views out there."

He shook his head as he buttoned his jeans. "Nope. None. "

"Not even from the sky?"

"No." His eyes bore into mine. "Nothing beats the view of you."

"Now I don't believe you." I slipped back into my shoes.

"Why not?" He looked adorable standing there half dressed with his hair disheveled. It was messy because of me, which made it so much better.

"Because for you nothing will ever be better than flying."

"That's not true. That," he gestured to the bed, "that beat flying."

I smiled. "So it wasn't just amazing on my side?"

"You knew it was amazing on my side too." He put on his shoes.

"Ok, I did." I grinned. "You made your enjoyment

known."

He ran a hand down my back. "Exactly."

"All right, let's do this." I unlocked and pushed open the door.

He wordlessly took my hand as we headed up the steep stairs to the deck. I wasn't looking forward to seeing the Allures again, but we didn't have a choice. We had to face reality before we spent any more fun time together.

"Get some sleep?" Violet grinned.

"No." Owen entwined his hand with mine.

"Not even going to pretend?" she asked.

"There's no point." I wasn't embarrassed about what Owen and I did. I was done taking life for granted, and if that meant having mind blowing sex with Owen while others knew it, that was fine by me.

"Put this on." Hugh tossed a shirt at him.

"Thanks." Owen pulled on the t-shirt.

I leaned in. "Now you ruined my view."

Hugh smirked. "You're ridiculous."

I shrugged and looked out at the seemingly endless water. We were surrounded by the calm blue water all around us, with no land in sight. "It's peaceful out here."

"I'm surprised you noticed." Violet nudged me. "Ready to focus now that you slept?"

"It wasn't sleep I needed." It felt freeing to stop caring about what others thought. Fear of disapproval was one feeling I didn't need.

"Where are we?" Owen walked over to the railing.

"On a boat."

"Let me rephrase that. How much farther do we have to go?" Owen rested an elbow on the railing.

"Not much farther. We'll be there soon."

"We timed that well." Owen winked at me.

I laughed. "So what now? Want us to take over?"

Hugh shook his head without stepping away from the wheel. "No thanks."

"Don't you want rest?"

"No, we don't *rest* together often." Violet's eyes twinkled with amusement. Clearly she was talking about sex.

"Often?" I was also done feeling embarrassed by my questions. I wasn't getting answers any other way.

"It's not all that important."

"Sure it is. Do makers usually sleep with the Allures they create?" I couldn't imagine Violet and Hugh sleeping together. I had so many questions about Allures, but I hoped I'd never need answers to them.

"Not always, but often." Hugh remained at the wheel. I couldn't imagine him sleeping with his maker, Violet.

"Did you sleep with your maker, Violet?" I decided to ask. She still hadn't told me much about him.

A surprised expression crossed her face. "What do you think?"

"Why would you throw a question back at me?" I wasn't letting her off the hook that easily. I was asking her an easier question than many of the others I could ask.

"Because I can."

I leaned back against the railing. "Yes. I think you were."

"I'm curious what you'll think of him."

"Of who?" Had I missed something?

"My maker."

"Will I meet him?" I knew nothing about him.

"Yes." She smiled lightly.

"Oh. When?"

"Later on. You'll meet some of our other friends first though."

"Other friends?" Owen asked suspiciously. "I think we've met plenty of your friends already."

"These aren't Allures. I'm curious what you'll think of them."

"What are they?" Owen shifted his weight.

"Dragos." Violet studied her nails. "Ever hear of them?"

"Dragos?" Owen's eyes bugged out. "I guess I should have known they were still around too."

Violet grinned and dropped her hand to her side. "Of course."

"Uh, what?" Not for the first time I was lost. I knew so little about the supernatural world.

"I'll explain later," Owen assured me before turning back to Violet. "Are they as bad as I've read?"

"I'm not sure bad is the right word." Violet turned to look out at the water.

"Ok, I'm done waiting." I put a hand on my hip. "What are Dragos?"

Violet smiled. "It's going to be easier to show you."

I looked at Owen. "Spill."

Owen nodded. "They're a shifter of sorts."

"Of sorts?"

"They are supposedly more like Pterons. Their shifted form is still humanoid."

"What animal are they tied to?"

"Ok, not really animal as much as a creature." He talked with his hands, something Owen never did.

"Come on. Spit it out."

"Dragons." Hugh shook his head. "I don't know why your lover boy won't just say it."

"Uh, what? Dragons?" Were there unicorns too?

Hugh laughed. "And they are just as much fun as they sound."

"Why do we need to see these friends of yours?" I still couldn't imagine a dragon version of a Pteron or whatever they were.

"They can help us get in a back way to Energo."

"Are they dangerous?"

Violet nodded without turning around. "Very."

I shivered.

"They won't hurt you. Dragos like Allures." Was my fear that obvious?

"But I'm not a full Allure yet."

She finally turned back. "You're close enough."

"And Pterons?" I asked.

"What, you don't think your Pteron can defend himself?" She smiled.

"Of course he can, but I wanted to know if they'll be friendly." I watched Owen out of the corner of my eye to make sure I hadn't unintentionally offended him. He didn't seem bothered.

"The Dragos are never friendly." Hugh opened a bottle of water and took a sip. "It's not in their nature."

"Never?"

He set down the water beside him by the wheel. "Well, except to certain Allures and a few others on rare occasions."

"Do certain Allures include Violet?" Everyone seemed to like Violet. I guess her cheerful personality got her a lot of fans.

"Yes, how'd you know?" She pulled out several bottles of water from a cooler and handed them out.

"Just a guess."

"They are only male, so they tend to be friendly to females of other creature types."

"How are they only male?" I knew enough about biology to understand how rare asexual animals were.

"They procreate with other species of females. It's simple really."

"What happens to the uh, women they procreate with?" From the way everyone was describing the Dragos I was a little nervous to hear the answer.

"They settle down with their mate for life."

"Oh…" Settling down with a dragon shifter? Hopefully their mates weren't human. I didn't know too many girls who would sign up for that life. But maybe they were like me and didn't have a choice in what happened to them.

"But it usually takes a Drago years to find a mate. Decades or centuries even. The Dragos we're seeing are all single. Once they mate they aren't around much."

"Oh…"

"And no they aren't having sex all the time." Hugh laughed.

"That's not what I was thinking." I adamantly denied it.

"Then what were you thinking?"

"Just. Ok, fine. It's what I was thinking." I felt blood rush to my face.

"And I wonder why sex is on your mind?" Violet nudged me again.

"Yeah, Daisy. I wonder?" Owen grinned.

"Changing subjects…" I wrapped my arms over my

177

chest. So much for not caring. I guess my bravado had worn off with the post-sex euphoria.

"Do you two want to be prepared?" Violet touched my shoulder.

"Of course we do." I dropped my hands to my sides and snapped out of my embarrassment.

"Do you want all the details even if they'll scare you?"

"It's always better to be prepared." I'd been left in the dark enough over the past few years.

"Not always." She hopped up onto the railing. My stomach did flips watching her, but she was calm. I guess taking risks weren't as scary when you were immortal. But did it really mean immortal? What happened to Taylor then? No one had actually said she was dead, but she had to be. I had her essence inside of me.

"Are you okay?" Violet looked over at me worriedly. "It looks like you just saw a ghost."

"No... nothing like that."

Hugh turned from the wheel. "She didn't mean that literally."

"I know. It's nothing."

"You sure?" Owen asked carefully.

Why did these thoughts and questions have to come to me at the worst times? We were close to reaching Energo, we were getting ready to meet some sort of half-dragon guys, and here I was ready to open up another can of worms.

"Just say it, Daisy. We know there's something major you want to say." Violet hopped down from the railing and stood in front of me.

"Allures are immortal." I made it a statement.

"In theory yes, but of course no creature is truly

immortal." Hugh looked at Owen. "Do you know how to drive this?"

"Yes." Owen took the wheel. I was surprised that he agreed so easily, but maybe he wanted Hugh to keep talking.

Hugh strolled over to me. "We are called immortal because our life spans last indefinitely, and we are immune to most means of death, but that doesn't mean that we can't be killed."

"Taylor." I let her name slip from my lips.

"And now we get to the real reason you asked." Hugh started to pace.

"Yes." I fought to keep my composure. I didn't want to appear more interested than necessary.

"We don't know how that happened."

"But it did. I mean I have her essence."

"You do… and so we know she may be dead, but we have no proof."

"Can an Allure live without her essence?"

"She wouldn't be an Allure then."

"Would she be human again?" Did that mean I'd still have a chance to remove the essence even if we were too late to stop the change?

"We don't know. It isn't something we've seen before."

"Ok… got it." I had so many more questions, but hopefully I wouldn't need answers. If things went my way I'd be walking away from the Allures and never looking back.

"Have we answered enough questions that you're ready for me to continue?" Violet tapped her foot impatiently.

"Yes. Go on. We were talking about being prepared."

"Yes. I was explaining that sometimes being prepared can hurt you."

"When can it?" Owen asked.

"When it scares you so much you can't function."

"This is going to be that scary?' I hoped she was talking big picture and not the current situation.

"Maybe." Hugh and Violet said simultaneously.

I leaned back against the rail again. "Fantastic."

"Nice sarcasm." Hugh smirked.

Violet smiled at me. "You and Hugh give each other such a hard time because you're meant to be friends. It's perfect."

"I have another random question." Why not try for one more?

"What is it?" Hugh asked.

"Where's Roland? He isn't in this realm. Does that mean he's back in the normal world?"

"The normal world?" Violet crossed her arms.

"You know what I mean."

"We don't know." Hugh returned to the wheel relieving Owen. I guess he was sick of the conversation.

Owen joined me by the railing. "Then why did you tell us that you persuaded him to stay back?"

"We did, but he wasn't where we left him."

"Why not?"

"If we knew we might have a clue where he is…" So much for Hugh exiting the conversation.

"He went missing?"

Violet nodded.

"How long has it been?" I needed to gauge a timeline.

"Not long. It hasn't been long since we met you."

"It feels like forever." It did. I could barely remember my life before returning to New Orleans. Was that a side effect of the change? The more they told me, the more questions I had.

"Where would he go?" That was the next logical one to ask.

"If we knew, we'd find him."

"He doesn't want to help me." That had to be part of the reason they didn't bring him.

"He thinks he's helping you."

"Letting me change isn't helping me. If he thinks it is, he's crazy." I let out a deep breath.

"He's not crazy. He's desperate. If you end up destroying his maker's essence… well, he loses the strongest personal connection he has."

"But even if I have it, I'm not her. We're not connected."

"Are you going to deny the effect he has on you? The way he calms you down?" Hugh turned to look at me.

"No, I'm not denying that, but I am denying that our connection is anything close to what he had with his maker."

"How would you know?' Hugh turned back around.

The boat started to heave up and down. "I guess I don't." I looked out at the suddenly choppy water.

"What was that?" Something flew by the boat. I braced myself on the railing and noticed two figures flying off in the distance.

"The Dragos have arrived," Violet said in a sing-song voice. Maybe she enjoyed the Dragos as much as they enjoyed her.

"Already?" I gripped the railing even tighter.

"Sometimes they get impatient." Hugh turned off the boat.

"Great." I took a few deep breaths. I wasn't sure what to expect from the Dragos, but that probably was a good thing.

I was learning paranormal creatures were never what you expected.

The silhouettes from the distance moved closer until they were right above us.

I held my breath as two men with long, powerful, leathery wings lined with spikes landed on the deck in front of us. The tan skin of their bare torsos was covered in an intricate pattern of tattoos. They were both wearing black pants and black boots.

Owen moved to my side.

"Why hello there," The first one grinned at me. His wings were lined with bright blue that matched his intense blue eyes. His black hair was cut short. While I stared, he retracted his wings. His bright eyes faded into a lighter shade of blue.

"Hello Troy, how nice of you to drop in." Violet held out her hand to him.

"Don't act surprised. We've had plans for a while." He took her hand and pulled her in so her body was flush against his. "And when will you learn to stop trying to shake my hand?"

"When will you learn that I prefer a more formal greeting?" Violet's voice was lighter, flirtier than usual. It made me uncomfortable, in the same way I couldn't stand watching my brother all lovey-dovey with a girlfriend. I wasn't sure why I even cared.

He stepped away and looked at me. "And who is this beauty?"

Owen stiffened at my side.

Violet smiled. "This is Daisy. Daisy, this is Troy, and that one," she gestured to the other winged creature. "That one is Wyatt." His wings had been lined in bright green that matched his eyes. When his wings retracted his eyes were a lighter shade too. Unlike Troy, he wore his equally dark hair longer.

"That one?" He put a hand to his chest. "Is that how you speak of me now?"

"I am merely introducing you."

Troy laughed. "Oh ex-lover spats. Aren't they a blast to witness?"

"Ex-lovers?" I asked with surprise. I'd have thought Violet had been intimate with Troy, not Wyatt.

"Don't listen to him, Daisy. Troy's only trying to rile me up." Violet rolled her eyes. "He'll fail."

Wyatt strode over to me and held out his hand. "Daisy, nice name. Why are you half-Allure?" He went straight to the point.

I didn't mind. "Uh, that's a long story."

He ran a hand through his black hair. "We have time. I'm guessing it has to do with why you need a ride to Mount Majest?"

"Yes."

"Wait. A ride?" Owen frowned "Why would Daisy need a ride?"

Troy rolled his shoulders back. The action accentuated the muscles in his strong arms. "Because climbing that mountain is impossible. You have to fly."

"I can fly. Daisy is covered." Owen took my hand.

"Oh my." Troy's lips twisted into a smile. "Are you one of those birds?"

"I'm a Pteron." Owen gritted his teeth.

"Listen, sweetheart, you can ditch the bird now. We're

here." Troy flashed his smile at me.

I wasn't sure if he was joking or not, but I wasn't going to wait before setting him straight. "Owen and I are together."

"Together?" Troy looked at Violet. "Has someone told her she can't actually be with anyone anymore?"

"Yes. That's why we're going to see the Elders."

"Wait." Wyatt looked between Owen and me. "No way, Violet. You aren't stupid enough to get the poor girl's hopes up."

"There is a chance. They may stop the change," Violet quickly replied.

Wyatt shook his head. "Delusional." He turned to me. "You will be an Allure. Don't let her fool you."

"I'm not giving up." I crossed my arms.

He rolled his eyes. "You're all delusional."

I walked over to the railing. There was nowhere else to go, but I couldn't look at anyone. I couldn't handle anyone else telling me I was doomed—or that everything would be okay. Things were what they were, but I wasn't ready to face the music.

eighteen

owen

The Dragos had to go. I could get Daisy to the Elders on my own. They were arrogant fools upsetting Daisy while at least one of them was simultaneously hitting on her. Neither was okay. "Daisy and I can take care of the rest on our own."

Violet shook her head. "You're not going to get an audience without me."

"I'll fly you both again then. I managed it fine last time."

"Daisy doesn't need a pet." Troy put an arm around Violet. She shrugged him off.

"I never said anything about bringing Glendale."

"Hey," The cat yelled. "I'm not a pet."

"I wasn't talking about Glendale," Troy ran a hand through his jet black hair. "I was talking about the bird."

"You little shit." I lunged for him, feeling transformation before I was even consciously aware. My fist made contact with his face.

"Stop!" Violet yelled.

I ignored her. He wasn't getting away with disrespecting me and my relationship with Daisy. I jumped on top of him, only to be immediately thrown off.

I looked up from where I'd been thrown on the deck to see Troy transformed. His wings flew out behind him, sharp spikes lining each one. He let out a large breath of smoke.

He smiled, crossed his arms, and retracted his wings as though we hadn't just been in a fight. He wiped blood off his face. "Impressive. You fight well for a bird."

I forced myself to transform back to my human form. I needed to stay calm. "Watch it."

"I'm complimenting you. I thought you were all city boys who couldn't defend yourselves. Maybe I was wrong."

"You were very wrong." I scowled. My dislike for Hugh was nothing compared to the way I felt about Troy.

"Enough of this testosterone fest." Violet stepped between us. "Let's focus on what's important."

I nodded. "Stopping the change." Taking care of Daisy was the priority.

"The quickest route from here into Energo is through the tunnel gate." Hugh crossed his arms. For his part he'd been quiet since the Dragos arrived. "I know none of you flying folks are going to like that though."

"We can stomach it if we move quickly." Wyatt frowned.

"What is the tunnel gate, and why are you two even coming?" The sooner we got rid of the Dragos, the better.

"Mount Majest is heavily guarded. Dragos have unlimited access due to a treaty," Violet explained.

"A treaty?" Daisy asked.

"We have some rather useful abilities." Troy grinned. "I'll have to show you some time."

The guy never learned. I had to fight down a growl. My Pteron side was fighting to come out again, and it was much more primal and uncontrollable than usual.

"Are we ready to do this?" Hugh pointed up toward the sky.

"Wait, we're stopping here?" Daisy narrowed her eyes. "I thought we had a ways to go."

"Flying will be way faster than the boat, and we have enough wings now."

"Perfect." Daisy grabbed hold of my hand. "Let's go."

"Are you sure you don't want me to fly you?" Troy grinned. "I promise I am faster."

"Absolutely." She straightened her shoulders.

I pulled Daisy against me. She was amazing. Completely and utterly amazing.

"We're going northwest. Follow my lead because we have to be careful where we land."

"Got it." I was anxious to get moving. I wrapped my arms around Daisy.

I waited for the Dragos to take off—Troy took Violet and Glendale, and Wyatt took Hugh.

As soon as they were in the air, I followed closely. We were finally getting to our goal, and I didn't want to waste a minute.

The flight was ten minutes, and I enjoyed every moment of having Daisy in my arms again. The last flight had been taxing, but this one was easy, and it helped put me at ease. The most surefire way to steady myself and stay calm was to fly. Add Daisy to the mix, and it was pure perfection.

I followed behind the Dragos and started my descent as soon as I saw them descend. I wasn't keen on anything involving tunnels, but I wouldn't be the only one uncomfortable in the confined space. They'd want to move through as quickly as I did.

We continued our descent through the clouds until finally the ground became visible. All I could see were ruins of old stone homes. Interesting spot to choose to land.

I landed on an old stone road, careful to make sure Daisy didn't feel any of the impact.

She looked around her. "Where are we? Was this once a city?"

By the multitude of crumbing rubble and the wide streets, I guessed this had once been a thriving city, but it was abandoned now.

"We are not here to sight see," Hugh snapped.

"I was just asking a question." Daisy bit her lip. "Something major happened here. I can feel it."

Violet took her hand. "You're nearly an Allure." She looked into Daisy's eyes. "You're feeling all the emotions of the people who were once here."

Tears streamed down Daisy's face. "I can feel the pain and anguish. It hurts so bad."

"That part will go away. You won't be able to feel it soon."

"She's not becoming an Allure." I pulled Daisy into my arms. "Let's get out of here. You heard her, it's hurting her."

"One day we'll tell you the story," Hugh spoke softly. "It's not one we have time for now."

"No, not if you want to get her to the Elders in time. I can barely sense the human in her anymore." Wyatt started to move down the deserted street.

I followed with Daisy tucked securely under my arm. She sobbed lightly, and I would have done anything to stop her pain.

"Remember these feelings are old. They aren't happening right now." Violet kept pace at Daisy's side.

"That doesn't matter. They feel real right now." Daisy buried her face in my side.

"Eventually you will understand time for what it really is. The pain you're feeling won't be there because you can't feel it in that way. It's a totally different sensation."

"But someone felt it. Someone felt this way."

"A long time ago. Way before your time." Hugh caught up.

"That means nothing to me."

"Then fight through it. Getting upset isn't going to help anything."

"I'm trying."

"You'll be fine once we enter the tunnel."

"*Violet.*" There was a warning in Hugh's tone. "Don't promise her that. The tunnel might be worse."

"Worse?" Daisy pulled her head up. "No. I'm not going through it then."

"We have to. There are no other entrances near here." Wyatt's tone was cold. From what I knew of Dragos they could feel, but then again I didn't even think they actually existed.

"Let's get it over with."

We continued down the worn stone road until Troy turned down a small alleyway.

I sincerely hoped they knew what they were doing. We moved down a sharp decline and walked underneath a bridge. Troy led us into what looked like an old storm drain. Wyatt and Hugh followed. Violet hung back with us.

"Are you ready for this?" I brushed some hair away from Daisy's face.

"Yes. We have no choice." She marched into the storm drain, and I followed holding on to her hand. Violet followed right behind me.

The pipe was dark, but there was enough light inside that my night vision worked. That was a big plus. The Dragos had no problem finding their way, so evidently they had night vision too.

Daisy whimpered.

"Are you okay?" I tightened my hold on her hand.

"It hurts."

"I told you." Hugh sighed.

Violet nodded. "I didn't think they'd be as strong in here, but they are."

"Think of all the people who tried to escape..." Hugh called back.

Daisy slunk down the floor, and I fell to my knees next to her. "Are you all right?"

She started to sob. I picked her up in my arms. The only thing that was going to help her was to move forward. The rest of the group seemed to understand, and we moved twice as fast the rest of the way through the pipe. We turned and entered a slightly wider tunnel.

"What was this tunnel for?" I hurried along behind the Dragos.

"Originally to move supplies," Troy explained.

"And later?"

"Escape and smuggling."

"I really wish someone would tell us where we are."

"Considering Daisy's condition, I wouldn't worry."

Violet's words were pointed.

"Agreed."

We continued down the tunnel until we reached a floor to ceiling gate that completely blocked our path.

"Please tell me one of you has your key." Violet pointed to the large padlock.

"I do." Wyatt inserted a small crystal key in the lock and pushed open the gate. All I could see was a hazy light, but I followed them through. As soon as Violet stepped through, she closed the gate behind her. We were still in a tunnel, but it had light seeping in through small cracks in the surrounding pipe. I already felt more comfortable, and Daisy's body felt less tense in my arms.

We continued through the tunnels until more and more sunlight filtered in. We finally reached the end and walked out into a valley full of bright green grass. We were surrounded by mountains, but one stood out from the rest. I craned my neck to take in the massive mountain that was so tall the peak was obscured by the clouds.

"It's 30,000 feet above sea level."

"That's twice as high as the highest peak in Colorado." My brief stay out there had made me appreciate mountains more.

"It's taller than Mount Everest. We weren't joking about this being a tall mountain." Violet looked up and smiled. "It's beautiful."

"It is." Daisy looked around. I still held her firmly in my arms. I didn't want to put her down until she was ready.

"We have to leave you here," Violet spoke carefully and directly to me. She did that a lot, but it wasn't going to help her this time.

"No. I'm not leaving Daisy." I hadn't come this far to be left behind.

"If it helps, I'll stay with you," Hugh offered.

"That doesn't help. I'm staying with Daisy."

"You can't." Wyatt transformed, his large wings spanning out behind him. "You must be invited first."

"Get me invited before she goes."

"Owen," Violet touched my arm. "Look at her."

I gazed down at Daisy's tired, yet absolutely beautiful face.

"She's running out of time."

"I can't trust you."

"You have to right now."

"You can put me down." Daisy ran her hand over my chest. "I can stand."

"Are you sure?"

"Yes."

I set her feet down gently on the ground next to me. "I don't want to make you do this on your own."

"She won't be alone. I'll be with her." Violet caught my eye.

"I can do this." Daisy seemed to be telling herself.

"Of course you can." Violet nodded. "But we need to go now."

"She'll be safe." Wyatt gestured for her to move toward him.

"One minute." She slowly walked toward me and kissed me lightly on the lips. "I love you."

"I love you too." Tears welled in my eyes and threatened to fall. I'd never felt so strongly about anyone or anything in my life.

"Always and forever." Tears streamed down her face.

"Always and forever." I forced myself to stay strong for her. Fighting and insisting I go would only slow things down. Violet was right. She was running out of time.

Wyatt and Troy took off with both of them, leaving Hugh, Glendale, and me in the valley. Watching Daisy fly off with Wyatt was one of the most difficult things I'd ever done. I was supposed to be with her, to protect her, but instead I was helpless.

"She's tough," Hugh glanced up to watch them fly off.

"Did I ask for your opinion?"

"No, but you should have. I have plenty of advice to give."

"None that I want."

"If things don't go your way today, you'll need it. I know how you can move on."

"I'm not moving on. Daisy is going to be okay." Losing confidence wasn't an option. She was going up there to face powerful creatures like none we'd ever seen. If she could do that, I could stay strong.

"You are not as bad as I originally thought." Hugh sat down on a boulder that stuck out of the thick grass at the foot of the mountain. Another one stood next to him.

"Is that because your expectations were low or because of something I've done?" I stayed standing.

"A little of both." He patted the boulder. "You should sit too. We are going to be here a while."

"That's just another reason to stand. I can't sit for long."

"We'll see what you are saying in a few hours."

"Hours? You think it's going to take that long?"

"Absolutely. Just hope it's not days."

"We don't have days."

"Exactly." He looked off into the distance.

193

nineteen

daisy

Flying with Wyatt was terrifying. I always felt safe with Owen, but Wyatt didn't put me at ease in the same way. He kept flying higher and higher, and all I could do was close my eyes. Owen was down there somewhere. He was waiting for me to come back to him as a human. I could do this. Everything would be fine if we could stop the change. We'd make it back home, and I'd see my family. Owen and I would make a life together.

I opened my eyes again, expecting to be close to the peak already, but we were only about halfway up. My ears hurt and my eyes burned, and I was already having difficulty breathing the thin air.

"You alive?" Wyatt asked over the wind.

"Kind of."

He laughed. "At least you still have your sense of humor."

"Just barely."

"It's something."

I closed my eyes again and thought of Owen. Soon I'd be back in his arms, and this experience would be a distant memory. Thankfully Wyatt didn't talk to me again. I could barely breathe, so talking wasn't going to work well.

Finally, what felt like hours later, he landed. I stumbled out of his arms, and nearly fell to the ground, but he caught me at the last second. "Take a moment. Regain your equilibrium."

"You make that sound easy." We were surrounded by clouds on all sides. I could barely see anything other than what was right in front of me. My breathing was labored.

"You're mostly Allure, so it should be easy."

"Mostly, but not completely."

"Things will be easier for you after the change."

Troy landed with Violet beside us.

"So I've heard."

"Daisy, you stay here with Troy and Wyatt. I'll be back." She started to walk away.

"Wait!" I followed after her.

She turned back around.

I stared at her with my mouth hanging open. "You're just going to leave?"

"I have to get us an audience. It will be easier this way."

"So what are we supposed to do?"

"Wait." She headed toward a spiral staircase that wound further up the mountain. I guess we weren't fully at the peak.

"Don't worry, you won't be alone." Troy smirked. He really wasn't my favorite person. Wyatt had been standoffish in the beginning, but I liked him a whole lot more.

"Great."

"I'll be back as soon as I can." Violet hurried off.

"So, what should we do?" Troy kicked a rock off the side of the mountain. An image of him kicking me off the mountain ran through my head, and I stepped further away from the edge.

"I'd never hurt you." He looked at me funny. "Don't be so dramatic."

"I never said you would." I straightened up as tall as I could. "I'm not worried."

"You were thinking about how I'd want to toss you off this mountain."

"I was not." I crossed my arms. What the hell? Was this guy reading my mind?

"Ok, sorry. More specifically you were worried about me kicking you off the mountain."

"How?" I was at a loss for words.

"Did you have to tell her already?" Wyatt groaned. "Now she's going to be all paranoid and try to hide her thoughts, which will only make them louder."

I rested my forehead in my hand. "I already had a headache."

"Get her some water," Wyatt instructed Troy. "Use the fountain."

"You get it yourself."

"She likes me better. You heard it as well as I did."

I was mortified. They'd heard me think that too? I felt blood rushing to my face.

"Don't be embarrassed. It happens."

"I'll be right back." Troy walked off the same way Violet had gone.

"This nightmare keeps getting worse."

"It's not a nightmare."

"No, because that would be too easy. I could wake up from a nightmare."

"This wasn't your choice?" He wrinkled his brow.

"No." I sat down on the rocky ground. My head was spinning from the altitude, and I was out of energy.

Wyatt sat down next to me. "That sucks. You should have had a choice."

"Were you born as a Drago?"

"Yes." He nodded. "The gene is dominant like with Pterons, so when a Drago finally mates any children are always Dragos."

"I do envy your ability to fly."

"You like wings." He raised an eyebrow.

"Yes, but I only love one set." I smiled.

"I can't tell you what he thinks."

"You mean you can't read his mind?"

"Nope. I'd heard Pterons were like that. We are too. I guess we're more similar than I thought."

"Did you also evolve? Like you used to turn into true dragons?"

"A long, long time ago."

"Cool. I like your form now. A lot of girls would find it attractive."

He laughed. "My guess is if you weren't in love with a Pteron you would too."

"What do those mean?" I pointed to the tattoos on his abdomen.

"They mark me as part of a clan."

"Oh?" My eyes traced over the winding design of black and grey that crossed his abs and continued around to his back. "Did you have them done when you were young?"

He scrunched up his face. "These aren't tattoos. I was born with them. All Dragos are born with a set. They are all a little different. Not a single set is the same."

"Like people. No two are the same."

"And snowflakes." He smiled. "I know you were thinking that first."

I buried my face in my hands. "Can I have no privacy?"

"You can. I can shut it off."

"Then why aren't you?"

"It takes some effort, and right now I need to keep my senses sharp."

"In case something happens."

"Exactly. If you get hurt, Violet is going to kill me."

"Can she?" I asked with real curiosity.

"Are you asking if I'm immortal?"

"Basically."

"In the same way an Allure is."

"How old are you?" I was asking more out of curiosity this time.

"Old."

"Old like Violet?"

"Older."

"What? Everyone acts like Violet is the oldest thing around!"

"Excuse me?" Violet's voice had me jumping.

I slowly turned around. "I didn't mean that in a bad way."

"I know." She held out a crystal goblet. "Drink this, it will help the altitude sickness."

"Great, all that work for nothing." Troy walked over holding a cup.

"That was thoughtful of you. Surprising even." She narrowed her eyes.

"Wyatt made me."

Violet nodded. "That makes more sense."

"How did it go? Did they grant us an audience?"

She nodded. "Drink this first, and then we'll get ready."

I sipped the cool liquid. It went down easy, and I drank more. I could breathe easier. "What do you mean get ready?"

"We both need to change."

"Why would we need to do that?"

"It's the rules." Troy rolled his shoulders back. "For everyone but us."

"What do we wear, and why don't you have to?"

"You wear robes, and remember the treaty and our powers."

"Do you have another ability besides mind reading?"

"Abilities and yes."

Violet's eyebrows drew together. "You know about the mind reading?"

"It slipped when she got worried about me kicking her off the side of the mountain."

She turned to me. "Did you actually believe I'd leave you with people who would hurt you?"

"Considering you dumped us alone on a deserted beach, maybe."

"That wasn't my fault. I assumed they'd come speak to us later."

I wasn't going to argue. "Where are these robes?"

"Inside." She gestured to the spiral staircase. "Let's go."

"Good luck." Wyatt smiled.

"You guys aren't coming?"

"No, this is Allure business."

"Okay." I followed her despite my nerves. There was no reason to put it off any longer.

twenty

daisy

My bare feet were cold as I walked across the marble floors of the palace. I understood removing my shoes out of respect, but wearing a white robe seemed a bit extreme even if Violet claimed it was an equalizer.

Although the robe covered me more than my usual clothes, I still felt naked. I took small and deliberate steps, purposely letting myself fall behind Violet. The bright white room felt endless, and maybe it was. I couldn't even see the ceilings because it was so tall, and other than the doorway I'd walked through, I hadn't seen another wall. Ahead of us all I could see was a bright light. It was so intense, I had to look at the floor in order to keep my eyes open.

I continued to follow Violet. Despite my concerns with her trustworthiness, she knew what she was doing, and she seemed to know the Elders. Staying behind her seemed like the safest option.

A shriek escaped my mouth before I realized what was

happening as someone grabbed my shoulder from behind. Once the momentary panic passed, I was hit by a wave of relaxation. I turned, not at all surprised to find Roland standing there.

He grinned as soon as our eyes met. "I've missed you."

I stared into his brown eyes at a loss for words. Why was he here? My headache returned. There was too much going on for me to handle. I turned back to find Violet facing us. She had her arms crossed over her chest.

She glared at him. "Interesting time to choose to show up."

"I couldn't let Daisy face the Elders without me. She has no maker, but I'm the closest thing she has to one. The question is why you think you had the authority to bring her here." He put his hands on my shoulders.

I tried to move out of his embrace.

Violet glowered. "I'm helping her."

"Helping her? No. You are trying to help yourself." Roland's hands tightened on my shoulders.

"How would this help her?" I thought back on everything Gabriel had said. The memories, her motive. Was it all coming to light?

"She still hasn't told you?" Roland spoke with his lips right next to my ear.

I struggled away from him. "Told me what?"

Violet shook her head. "Stop putting negative thoughts in her head. I'm here to help her. She wants to stay human. I want to help. We all willingly accepted the gift. She should have been given the choice too."

"Are you all done prattling?" A booming voice had me jumping for the second time in a few minutes.

"Yes." Violet linked her arm with mine and tugged me away from Roland. He easily caught up and took my other arm, reminding me of the first night we'd met. It felt like a lifetime ago.

My heart was beating a mile a minute as we walked toward the bright light. I couldn't see anything but the light, and that made things even scarier.

"It's fine. Everything is going to be okay," Violet whispered the soothing words into my ear.

"Just tell them the truth. Only the truth." Roland's words weren't nearly as soothing. Despite the comfort his touch gave me, his words sent shivers down my spine.

"I'll lead everything. Speak when you're asked direct questions. I will handle the rest." Violet pulled me closer.

"Be careful who you trust," Roland warned.

I felt like a ping pong ball being volleyed back and forth between Violet and Roland. I longed for Owen. He'd keep me focused. I shook my head. *No.* He'd be in danger. It was important I was doing this without him. I never wanted to put him at risk.

The light became brighter the closer we walked toward it. I continued to look down. The glare was so strong it hurt my eyes.

"Stay calm," Violet said quietly. "The worst thing you can do right now is get upset."

"Really?"

"Yes. The Elders will use your fear against you. Fear is your greatest weakness." She spoke in a breathless tone that made me question whether she was nervous too. And if she was, what did that mean? Was she going to turn on me?

We continued walking through the seemingly endless

room until we suddenly stepped through the light.

I blinked a few times.

"Now you don't see that every day, do you?" a low and sultry female voice said.

I looked up. The intense light had vanished. In front of us were ten men and women sitting in ornate golden chairs that resembled thrones. They may have been called Elders, but they didn't look it. Each was breathtakingly attractive and in their prime. Just like Violet. None looked to be over thirty. Each was dressed differently, in clothes that varied from formal wear to jeans. Evidently they had no dress code.

"Aren't you going to answer?" The blond woman sitting second from the right spoke again. "It's rude not to."

I looked at Violet. She gestured for me to talk. "You were speaking to me?"

"Do you usually answer questions with questions?"

"No." It took every ounce of strength I had to talk. I'd never felt so intimidated in my entire life.

"Then say something." She made it sound so simple.

"I don't even understand what you asked." My head spun. I had never remembered feeling so confused.

"Permission to speak, Arabella?" Violet's voice was strong and unwavering.

"Granted." Arabella nodded.

Violet cleared her throat. "Daisy has had a lot to digest in the past few days. Please forgive her difficulty responding."

"I still do not understand your presence here." Arabella crossed her legs.

"I am here to champion her cause."

"Isn't that her maker's job?" She gestured to Roland.

Violet held up her chin. "He's not her maker."

"Yet they share part of an essence. How is that possible?" Arabella shifted in her seat, revealing more of her elegant black gown.

"She was given an Allure essence against her will." Violet's face was expressionless. I braced myself. How would these people react?

They looked horror struck. "How do you know it was against her will?" one of the men asked.

Another Elder jumped in next. "Do you take the child's word as truth?"

Child? Maybe compared to them.

"It was the result of misguided witchcraft. The residue was still on her when we met her." Roland stepped in front of me. "I can assure you she did not willingly take the essence."

"I couldn't imagine she'd be able to. She doesn't appear particularly strong." A male elder sized me up and evidently wasn't impressed. First a child and now weak. These people were not flattering me at all.

"Tell us the story." The man directly in front of me leaned forward in his chair. "I want to hear it from you."

"From me?" I put a hand to my chest. I could barely concentrate let alone tell them anything.

"Again with the questions." Arabella rolled her eyes.

"Yes, you." The man tapped his foot impatiently. "Tell us the story."

"There isn't all that much more to tell."

"I'm sure there is." He rested his inhumanly muscular arm on the armrest of the chair.

"I was given a magic paste by a witch that had Allure essence in it."

"Start before that. From the beginning." He wove his

hand around.

"The beginning was taking a road trip to New Orleans with my roommate at the time. She wanted to reconnect with her ex-boyfriend, and I stupidly went along for the ride." I liked to blame it on being young.

"And what happened?"

I decided to skip over the part about getting felt up by Shaun. "I got bored and was wandering around in the French Quarter and found a Voodoo shop."

"You simply happened upon it?" The man asked.

"No. A photographer recommended I check it out."

"Who was the photographer?"

"Harold something. He had a shop on Royal Street, but he's not there anymore. I met his son though."

"Based on the suggestion of a complete stranger you walked into a Voodoo shop." The elder didn't hide his disbelief.

"It was a tourist trap kind of place. It's not like I went to a witch's house or anything."

"Continue." He waved me on.

"The witch said she had just the thing for me, and she put the paste on my forehead. She called it Seduction's Kiss."

"Again, you allowed a woman you didn't know to put a paste on you?" Instead of disbelief, his expression had become one of disapproval.

"I was young and stupid. Is that what you want to hear?"

"No. I don't want to hear anything but the true story."

"Yes, I allowed it. I thought it was just a touristy thing."

"What happened next?"

"I went out on Halloween night with a guy who turned out to be a vampire stripper."

The elder raised an eyebrow. "A vampire stripper?"

Arabella laughed, and the man gave her a stern glare.

"I apologize, Abe." She bowed her head. Evidently he was the leader.

"Yes. And he introduced me to more vampires, and I ended up being dragged back to their nest in a body bag. As did my friends."

"And what did they do to you at their nest?" Arabella appeared more interested now. I guess I was entertaining her.

"The leader tried to drain me, but I was saved by a Pteron." I smiled thinking of Owen.

"A Pteron happened to find you?" Abe raised an eyebrow.

"It turns out he'd noticed me previously, although he hadn't shown it."

"So you'd met the Pteron before?" Arabella asked.

"Unofficially." I started to sweat. I felt like I was standing under hot lights.

"Why didn't you tell us?" Abe questioned. "I told you we needed the full story."

"I didn't think that mattered."

"The whole truth means the whole truth, not the things you think are important." Abe leaned back in his chair.

"Well, then I was also felt up by the roommate of my friend's ex. Is that important?"

He nodded. "Maybe to your state of mind."

"I don't want to be this." I gestured to myself. "I want to be human. I want to go back to my normal life." I'd had enough of the interrogation. I needed to know if I had a chance of convincing them to help.

"But with Owen." Roland grunted.

"Who's Owen?" Arabella asked.

"Her Pteron savior. Whom she professes to love." Roland's voice dripped with sarcasm.

"Something else she failed to mention." Arabella tapped her nails on her armrest.

"I hadn't gotten that far."

"You had. You were telling us you wanted to go back to your normal life."

"Why don't you want the gift?" Another male elder addressed me. "Doesn't immortality and power appeal to you?"

I shook my head. "Love and happiness appeal more."

"Love of this Pteron?" Abe questioned.

"Yes, and my family."

"But does this Pteron even love you?" Arabella asked with a hint of a smile. "Maybe he finds you amusing, a fun distraction. Is he worthy of your love?"

"Yes." I didn't hesitate. I knew his feelings were genuine, and he was definitely worthy. "He loves me, and I love him."

"How do you know he loves you?" Arabella leaned forward.

"Because he's waiting for me in the valley. He came all the way here for me."

"Are you sure? Maybe he had other reasons to desire entry to our home." Arabella caught Abe's eye.

"He didn't. I'm tired of people trying to convince me of everyone else's ulterior motives. Some people actually do things because they care."

"Like Violet?" Roland turned to me. "You still think that's why she's here?"

"That doesn't really matter. She's here. She brought me here. In the end that's what matters."

"Is it?" Roland's eyes were cold as he leaned in close to whisper in my ear. "What if the Elders won't help you because of her?'"

I let out a deep breath. I could handle this. "The Elders' decision to help me or not will have little to do with Violet."

"Correct. You do have intelligent things to say when you stop asking questions." Arabella beamed at me.

I jumped at the opening. "Can you stop the change? Can you make me human again?"

"They won't destroy the essence. They can't." Roland turned his back to me.

"You are both right." Abe caught my eye. "We can stop the change, but we must not destroy the essence."

"Then what will you do?" Violet asked calmly.

"That depends." Abe kept his eyes on mine.

"Depends?"

"On how much Daisy and what was the Pteron's name?" He waved his hand again.

"Owen," I quickly supplied.

"Owen. On how much Daisy and Owen value their love."

"What do you mean?" I asked nervously.

"I don't remember my human life well, but I remember love." Abe leaned back and broke eye contact. "I will know the real thing when I see it."

"It's real." I stepped toward the elders. "It's completely real."

"I'm sure you think so, but I'll have to see you together."

"I'll get him." Violet nodded.

"Wait, you're leaving already?" I wanted her to get Owen for me, but I felt nervous about being left alone.

"I'm here." Roland smirked. "Why would it matter if she

left?"

"Because you don't want me to stop the change. You aren't on my side." I stomped my foot.

"I'm always on your side." His expression didn't change.

"I won't be long, if permission to bring the Pteron is granted." Violet bowed slightly.

"Permission granted." Abe nodded. "But use haste."

"I will." Violet hurried out of the room.

"I would like to talk to the girl alone." Arabella stood up. "Come with me."

"Now?" I'd been hoping to wait for Owen. I couldn't wait to see him and prove we were truly in love. They'd have to see it. It was so strong anyone would be able to.

"Yes, what other time would I mean? You really should stop asking questions." She flipped her long blond hair off her shoulder.

"Okay."

I followed the tall woman, she was well over six-feet, away from the chairs. She walked outside into a courtyard area.

"Have you thought things out? Are you sure you know what you're doing?" She stopped in front of a stone fountain situated between two Japanese maple trees.

"I don't want to change."

"But why? And do you understand what you'll be giving up?" She sat on the edge of the fountain. "Although you did not initially consent to become an Allure, you should be fully informed before you decide to forgo your gift."

"No offense, but being an Allure doesn't excite me as much as it seems to excite everyone else."

"Sit," she ordered.

"Ok." I sat down next to her, leaving plenty of space.

She nodded in approval. "Has anyone explained the power?'

"The manipulation?" It wasn't a good ability to have. "Yes."

"There's more than that. So much more than that. So many secrets left to share with you." Her eyes twinkled.

"I don't want to know the secrets."

"Yes you do." She leaned toward me. "I can tell. It's in your eyes, in the way you hold yourself. You're desperate to know more, to fully change, but you're scared."

I shook my head. "I'm not giving up my humanity."

"Why? Because of a Pteron who will forget you? For your family you've barely mentioned? What reasons?" She crossed her legs.

"For those and more. I have my whole life left to live." I stood up. "My whole life."

"And being an Allure will be more than a life. It will be an eternity. You can live any life you want over and over," she jumped to her feet.

"It doesn't count if I'm not human. It doesn't count at all." Nothing she could tell me would change my mind.

"Why not? What is it about being human that makes it different?" She leaned back on her hands.

"Everything."

"Like?" She twirled hair around her perfectly manicured finger.

"Being able to feel. What's the point of experiencing anything if you can't feel it?" I'd never thought about the importance of emotion before I started to change, but now it was everything. I realized I would be nothing but a shell of myself without it. No one would be.

"You can still feel things. You can still feel the adrenaline rush when you jump out of a plane. You can still feel the heat of the sun when you lie on the beach. You can smell the intoxicating scents of exotic cuisines. You can feel the wind, hear the birds." She stood and twirled around like a child.

"But that isn't emotion. That's not what I mean."

"The surge from manipulating replaces your need for emotions. I promise. Who needs their own joy, when you can use it?" She smiled broadly. "It's better that way. You can choose what emotions you touch and experience. The power and control is in your hands."

"It matters to me. I want to feel joy and love. I even want to feel pain if it's for the right reasons. That's what being human means, and that's who I am."

She shifted her weight from one high heeled clad foot to the other. "Sex is still sex when it's with your maker, or the one you make." She ran her teeth over her lip. "In case that's what's holding you back."

Had she been listening to a word I said? Did she really think it was all about sex? Even if it was, which it wasn't, she was wrong. "Physically, but not emotionally."

"With your maker it's emotional. It's one of the few exceptions."

"I don't have a maker." And everyone knew it. That's what made my situation so strange and made me wonder if they really would ever welcome me into the fold as an Allure.

"Not technically, but you share the bond with Roland. It will work the same way." She stepped toward me. "He knows it. Why do you think he's being so pushy?"

"That has nothing to do with it, and either way, I don't

want to have sex or be with anyone but Owen."

"Why?" She seemed genuinely curious.

"Because I love him."

"Why? And is that love truly stronger than your desire for immortality?" She sat back down in the same spot she'd been in. I hoped she didn't ask me to sit, because I couldn't. I had too many nerves coursing through me to sit down.

"Yes. I have no desire to live forever. None."

"Everyone does to some degree."

"I don't. I don't want to die now. I want to live a long life and grow old. With Owen. I want to have children and grandchildren and watch them grow older." Having kids wasn't something I planned to do soon, but it was still something I wanted someday.

"Why?" She leaned in. "Do you say that because it's what you think you're supposed to say?"

"No, it's what I know. What I feel."

"But your feelings are just that. Feelings. They are fleeting and easily changed." She glanced behind her into the pool of the fountain. She smiled, and I realized she was checking her reflection.

"I don't want to live forever, and I don't want to live if I can't feel."

She turned back around. "You're going to change your mind."

"I'm not." I crossed my arms. The action reminded me I was standing in a simple white robe. Why was I wearing this while Arabella was dressed to the nines?

"If we stop the change, you'll regret it. You'll spend the rest of your dismal short life wondering 'what if'. 'What if' you had taken the chance?"

"No." I shook my head. "I'd always regret if I did change."

She laughed dryly. "Now we both know that's not true. You won't feel regret as an Allure."

"And that changes everything?"

"Yes." She stood.

"Please stop the change. I'll do anything." I wasn't above groveling at her feet if it would help.

"Be careful what you offer."

"I already told you I'd rather die than lose the ability to feel." I wasn't suicidal. I'd never do that to the people in my life, but I wouldn't be me if I changed. I wasn't about to spend thousands of years roaming the earth as a paranormal creature that manipulated people, even destroyed their lives, on a whim. It couldn't happen. That wasn't me at all.

"Do you want to see?"

"See what?"

"What your life could be?"

"What do you mean?"

"Do you ever stop asking questions?"

"Not when my life and future are on the line."

"Answer me. Do you want to know?"

"I don't understand what you are even asking. What are you offering to show me?"

"The future."

"You can see into the future?"

"I can show you."

"I don't want to know." The decision came swiftly, and I stormed back inside. Some things were better left unseen.

twenty-one

owen

I practically ran inside the palace. Violet had to grab my arm to slow me down, and even then I was tempted to brush her off. I needed to get to Daisy. Violet had assured me she was fine, but how would she even know? She'd been gone awhile to come get me.

I'd accepted the simple white robe without protest. I'd have walked around naked if it meant seeing Daisy. As soon as the doors open I sprinted across the infinite marble floors of the palace.

"Owen!" Daisy ran toward me with her dark hair falling down her back. I pulled her into my arms and let my lips immediately find hers. I didn't care about the audience. We were together, and that was all that mattered.

"Are they always like this?" A male voice asked.

Daisy broke the kiss, and I reluctantly pulled away. I satisfied myself by slipping her hand in mine before we continued toward the semi-circle of thrones that seated the

Elders.

"Usually. They are rather lovey-dovey." Violet smiled.

"We have never had a Pteron inside this palace."

"I appreciate the grant of an audience. I would do anything to secure Daisy's human nature." I kept my voice even and calm even though my heart was racing.

"You did it too. Promising anything? That's a dangerous promise to make." An attractive blonde stood from her throne and walked toward us. "I would have thought your king would have taught you better."

"My king taught me to stand up for what I believe in and protect those I love with every ounce of strength I have." I intended to do both no matter what it cost me.

"Daisy is agreeing to decline the greatest gift imaginable, immortality and power beyond your wildest dreams." The apparent leader stepped down and joined the blonde.

"She knows what she wants." I squeezed her hand.

"But would you do the same? Would you give up your greatest gift?" The leader studied my face.

"Yes." I didn't waver.

"That's what love is about it, isn't it? Sacrifice." He stood completely still in front of us.

"That's part of it, but it's so much more." I kept eye contact, wanting him to understand there wasn't a chance I would step down.

"But sacrifice is always part of it. Whether it's a small sacrifice of where or how to live, or a big one, like who and what you will be."

"We both agree we'd do anything to save her ability to feel."

"But do you really mean it?" He leaned in toward me.

"Yes. I would give my life." That reality shook me to my core, but it was true. I'd risk anything to protect her.

"But life isn't your greatest gift. You weren't given immortality."

"No, and I never asked for it." Living forever didn't appeal to me. I'd miss my friends and family too much.

"But you were given other gifts."

"Yes." I wondered what he was thinking.

"The biggest gift is hiding under that robe." The blonde walked behind me and slipped down my robe, running her finger down my back.

That's when it hit me. *My wings.*

"Would you give your wings up?" The blonde moved back around in front of us. "Would you give up the ability to fly?"

"No!" Daisy's yell echoed through the room.

I ran my thumb over Daisy's hand to calm her down. "If that's what it takes." I'd always thought my wings made me who I was, but I was wrong. I was more than a Pteron. I was a man, and I had a heart. "I would give my wings for a guarantee that Daisy would stay human, and we could live a life in peace."

"No! Don't listen to him. He doesn't know what he's talking about!" Daisy yelled. She tried to pull her hand from mine. "You can't do this, Owen. You'll regret it, and you'll end up hating me. I'm not worth it." Tears streamed down her face.

I took both of her hands in mine. "It's completely worth it. You're worth it and our love is. I told you we'd love each other forever, and I meant it."

"No." She shook her head. "Not that."

"She's right." Roland walked over. I'd been so focused on Daisy and the Elders that I hadn't noticed him. "You'll regret it and hate her forever. Is that what you really want?"

"Shut up." I glared at him. "You want her to stay an Allure. Your opinion means nothing."

"I want her to have happiness, but I agree with them both." Violet closed her eyes for several seconds before opening them as though she were preparing for something. "You will regret it, just as Daisy would always regret losing her chance to be an Allure."

"You're supposed to be helping us." My hands balled into fists. "Now you're going to turn against us?"

She shook her head. "I also told Daisy I'd protect you. This is protecting you both. You'd regret it, and you'd eventually despise her. What kind of life would that be?"

"It won't happen. I could never hate her."

"I could show you." The blonde held out her hand. "I can show you exactly what will happen."

Violet stepped between us. "No. If you watch the future, it will come to pass. It can't be changed."

The blonde glared at her. "Do you wish to spend the next century locked up? Weren't three decades enough?"

Violet paled. "These years don't matter nearly as much as those did."

"Violet." The leader cupped her chin in an intimate way that only lovers do. "You know I never want to see you suffer again."

"Then don't allow the boy to make such a stupid decision."

"It is his stupid decision to make. If he's so in love, then let him do it. We'll take the essence back and give it to someone more worthy."

"It won't be easy." Another elder stood up. "It's harder and harder to find a human who can accept the gift anymore."

"She still gets the choice. It's the ultimate rule. He gets a choice too."

"Our choice is made." I knew without a shred of doubt what my answer was. "We are ready to give up our gifts if it means we can be together."

"No!" Daisy pleaded.

"Let's give them time." The leader gestured and all of the Elders stood. "We will vacate the room. When we return, you need to have your answer."

"We already have it." I didn't need time. I wanted the change stopped, and I wanted everything done. I wanted it over with.

"Daisy wants time." The leader took Violet's hand and led her toward the door. He looked at Roland. "You must leave them too."

"Yes." Roland nodded and followed the line of Elders outside.

"My decision is made." I didn't give Daisy a chance to argue. She had a guilt complex, it's all this was. We belonged together, and I was willing to do anything to make sure that happened.

twenty-two

daisy

I had no real choice. Only one answer was acceptable, yet giving it meant losing everything and anything I cared about. It meant losing Owen, and it meant losing myself.

"Daisy?" Owen looked deep into my eyes.

"I love you." I didn't think, I didn't question. I crushed my lips against his, needing to soak up his taste and feel. He responded immediately, deepening the kiss as he wrapped me up in his arms.

Always and forever. Our promised words swirled through my head. Promised words that couldn't possibly be true. But in that moment it didn't matter. The truth couldn't hurt us. Only time could.

"Daisy?" He broke the kiss and looked into my eyes again. "You understand, don't you? You understand I am more than willing to give up flight for you."

I nodded. "I understand, but that doesn't mean it's right."

"Of course it's right. We're right." He rested his hands on

my hips. My body warmed to his touch, but I fought to stay strong.

I closed my eyes, I was about to hurt the only man I'd ever loved. The only man I would ever love. "This isn't love."

"What do you mean?" Confusion crossed his face. "Even the Elders saw it. It's the truest love there could ever be."

I shook my head and fought back the tears. "We barely know each other. It's not love, Owen. It's only lust. And because of that I can't let you make the biggest mistake of your life."

"That's a lie." He gritted his teeth. "Take it back. You know as well as I do that it's love."

I did, but I couldn't admit it. I couldn't give myself any room to back down. Abe was right. Love involved sacrifice, and sometimes the greatest sacrifice was letting someone go even when you wanted to hold on to them more than anything. "I have to go."

He captured my wrist as soon as I turned. "No. You can't leave. We're almost out of time. We have to do this now."

"It's too late, Owen. I've made up my mind." My heart broke, but I had to say the words. I had to convince him to save his wings. They meant more to him than me even if he couldn't see it yet.

"No. It's not your choice." He shook me. "Stop this. I'm the one giving up the wings. It's my choice."

"I don't want you making the choice. I already told you. It's lust." The dam of tears broke, and I fell to the floor. I'd never kiss him again. I'd never know the intense passion we shared. I'd never know any passion.

"Daisy, stop this." His eyes widened. "Stop this now."

"Do we have a decision?" Abe and Violet walked back in.

I nodded, forcing up the courage to do what was right. "I changed my mind. I want to be an Allure."

Understanding crossed Violet's face. "Come with me, Daisy. Everything is going to be okay."

"No. Daisy you can't do this!" Owen grabbed for me.

Abe pushed him back. "You heard her. She changed her mind. Your audience is over. Troy will escort you back to your home realm immediately."

"Daisy, no." Owen shook his head and tears slid down his face. "Please, don't do this."

I ran from the room into the courtyard. I couldn't face him. I couldn't see the pain I caused the man I loved, but I knew I was doing the right thing. I still had the ability to feel, to make decisions based on my emotions. Owen couldn't be separated from his wings. They were what made him who he was. I'd rather live eternity without him than watch him suffer. He deserved better. He'd find better.

"It's going to be okay." Violet put a hand on my shoulder. I shrugged her off. It wasn't going to be okay, and it would hurt until the change happened completely. Then I could finally hide inside my emotionless existence.

My brief time with Owen had changed me, and I hoped I'd one day be granted a glimpse back at the beautiful moments we'd shared. I would do everything possible to find my way back to myself, but I knew that was only a pipedream. My human life was over, and that meant any life with Owen.

"Daisy!" Owen called my name again from somewhere in the distance, and I curled up into a ball on the ground.

"Please, can you make the change come faster?" I'd never imagined I'd ask for something like that, but I needed it. The pain was too much to bare.

lust

"Yes." Arabella's voice came from behind me. "We can make it instant, Daisy. All you have to do is ask."

"Do it." I closed my eyes and waited for the feelings to fade away.

Owen and Daisy's story continues in
Lost (The Allure Chronicles #3), coming soon.

Keep reading for a preview of
Forged in Stone (The Forged Chronicles #1),
a New Adult Fantasy Romance by Alyssa Rose Ivy

www.AlyssaRoseIvy.com
www.facebook.com/AlyssaRoseIvy
twitter.com/AlyssaRoseIvy
AlyssaRoseIvy@gmail.com

To stay up to date on Alyssa's new releases, join her mailing
list: eepurl.com/ktlSj

Forged in Stone
The Forged Chronicles
Alyssa Rose Ivy

The son of darkness is all grown up...

James is a Guardian. He is tasked with protecting the most important person in his world. For eight years he has done his job without complaint, but he has grown tired of living under the shadow of a father who is responsible for the most unimaginable violence and destruction his world has ever known.

Ainsley is at a loss for what to do with her life. She hates her two dead end jobs and the family who betrayed her. She has resigned herself to living one day at a time, but she longs for an escape from her lonely life.

When Ainsley finds James in her bed, their two lives and worlds collide. They may have both found exactly what they need, but the darkness James has been running from his whole life has just caught up.

James

The dated rock music was giving me a headache. If not for the alcohol still left in my glass I would have been out of the bar already. Even the redhead hanging on my every word was getting to me. Did girls no longer believe in the chase?

"James?" she said my name with an exaggerated southern drawl that came across as almost fake. It probably was.

"Yes?" I blinked a few times trying to bring things back into focus. I had drunk far too much, but there was nothing I could do about that now.

"Are you even listening to me?" She tapped her fingers on the bar top between us.

"No." I took in the faded blue paint on the walls. The place had seen better days, but it served my needs perfectly. No one thought anything of the quiet guy getting plastered at the bar. I blended in.

"I asked you if you wanted to take me home. I only live a few blocks from here." She put her hand on my upper thigh.

I looked into her glazed over green eyes. "Probably not."

"Oh." Hurt marred her overly made-up face, and for a second I felt bad, but then it faded. She would be even more hurt when I left her in the morning. Besides, if she was half as drunk as I was, she had no idea what she was asking.

"I am doing you a favor." I downed the rest of my beer. It was some crappy lager I had no plans to try again. I had chosen it as an alternative to the whiskey that had filled my glass earlier in the evening.

"Oh." She stared at me blankly. She clearly liked that word.

"See you around." I moved over a stool to make sure she got the less than subtle hint. I did not particularly enjoy being mean, but I had no time or energy to play nice.

Loud laughter got my attention. "Cold."

I looked at the aging bartender chuckling in front of me before glancing down at the now vacant stool the redhead had been seated on. "Honesty."

"You have to admit that was harsh." He leaned on his elbows. "Do you usually treat pretty girls that way?"

"Would it have been better to have bedded her and never spoken to her again?"

He straightened up. "No, but there is an in-between. There is value in politeness."

"And what value is that?" I pushed my empty beer glass toward the bartender. "Give me something stronger this time."

"I can't serve you more. We both know that."

"And we both know you make exceptions." I was drunk.

There was no question about that, but I needed more to numb the emptiness. Otherwise there was no point in having made the trip into Charleston.

"I can't serve you more booze, but I don't mind listening."

"Listening?" I raised an eyebrow. "Do I look like I want someone to listen?"

"You're wasted before nine o'clock at night. You need someone to talk to."

"Next time I will wait until later to get intoxicated." I tossed down enough money to cover double my tab and stumbled out of the bar.

The cool night was a welcome change from the stifling heat of the overcrowded dive. It had been years since I lived in the city of Charleston, South Carolina, but one thing remained the same. They still insisted on pumping heat into buildings the second the temperature dropped south of sixty degrees. I doubted that most of the people at the bar could survive long where I came from.

The city portion of my walk should not have taken long, but it did. I guess that happens when you get pissed drunk. I knew Charleston well from the months I lived there in high school—and the few nights I spent there now. I spent most of my time in an altogether different place, a place that had stopped feeling like home years ago. A place that was literally another world.

I was far too exhausted to make it all the way back home, so I stopped at the one place I could in the city. I had no key, but I had another plan to get in. I went around back, taking one cursory look into the withering garden before starting my climb up the thick ivy that wound its way all the way up to the third story balcony.

The ivy swayed under my weight, but I made it onto the balcony without breaking my neck. I shook the doorknob with enough force to get it to budge. I pushed the door open, kicked off my boots, and tossed my shirt before collapsing on the queen sized bed. It was not my bed, but at the moment any bed would do.

Chapter
TWO

Ainsley

I was living the life of a TV sitcom friend. You know the type: the boring one that serves no purpose except to make the main character seem more interesting. I worked not one, but two dead end jobs. I didn't know which was worse, serving frozen yogurt or working as an office assistant at a law firm. Neither had anything to do with my career goals, but as my mom always said, beggars can't be choosers. My art history degree had proved as useful as it sounded. I couldn't manage to land a job working in a gallery, let alone a museum. I'd eventually have to go back to school to get a degree in something useful, but the thought of spending time in a classroom wasn't something I could stomach. At twenty-two, I was just happy to be paying the bills without moving back in with my parents. It was more than most of my friends could say. Or at least most of the friends I still had.

I waited impatiently as a couple stared at the flavor listing above my head. They'd been in the frozen yogurt shop for twenty minutes already. We only offered a dozen flavors. The decision couldn't have been that hard to make. "We close at nine." I used the most polite voice possible, but as it was 8:56 I figured they needed a reminder.

"That means you don't let new customers in after nine. We're already here. You can't kick us out." The guy wrapped his arm around his date's waist. "Don't worry baby, there's no rush."

I bit my tongue. Who did this clown think he was? If I wasn't certain the guy would report me and get me fired, I would have given him a piece of my mind. Instead I started wiping up a sticky spot on the counter I'd overlooked earlier. Despite how boring the job was, it did pay decently, and I didn't mind my boss.

"Can I try the vanilla again? I'm not sure I liked it." The girl pointed at the hard yogurt in the case in front of her.

Seriously? Who tried vanilla twice? I mean everyone in the world knew what that flavor tasted like. I gritted my teeth. "Sure." I picked up one of the small pink spoons and scooped a tiny amount. I handed it to her.

She tasted it. "I'm still not sure."

I glanced at the neon colored clock by the door. It was two minutes after nine now. "I'm sorry, but I really have to close."

"No you don't. You're going to let my girlfriend take her time and pick a flavor." The guy puffed out his chest like that was supposed to intimidate me or something.

I sighed before glancing at the clock again. I was going to be late meeting my friends for drinks. Or really my friend

Grace and her other friends. Saying it in the plural made it sound better.

"Is the chocolate chip cookie dough flavor good?" The girl batted her long eyelashes. I'd have bet a lot they were fake.

"If you like cookie dough, yes."

She nodded as though I'd just shared some life altering secret. "Can I try that one too?"

I sighed again. "Sure." I took out another pink spoon.

She tried it. "I changed my mind. I don't want anything." The girl turned toward the door.

"I agree. Horrible service here." The guy followed her and slammed the door behind him.

I silently cursed them while I wiped down the rest of counter. There was a time in my life when I got along with everyone. That time had come and passed. Now I was lucky if I could handle being in the same room as someone who rubbed me the wrong way. It made working in the service industry dicey, especially when your customers were mostly tourists. I loved living in Charleston, but sometimes I wished I lived somewhere a little more off the beaten path.

I finished my clean up and checked the clock again. I didn't have time to do much to help my appearance, but I changed into a black three-quarter length sleeve sweater rather than my Yogurt Love t-shirt. I checked the tip jar. There wasn't much in there, which was the same way it was every shift. Clearly my sparkling personality wasn't doing me any favors.

I locked up and hurried out to my car, checking the clock as soon as I started the engine. Nine twenty-two. I could still make nine-thirty if I didn't hit too many lights.

I raced down to King Street, nearly destroying my car in an attempt to parallel park in the smallest spot known to man. Even my tiny Honda Fit barely found enough room. If it had been during the day, I could have avoided using my car completely, but I was far too paranoid to walk around the city alone at night. My step-dad the cop had shared countless horror stories with me.

I got out and booked it around the corner to the bar. Right before I reached the entrance I realized I hadn't locked the car. I turned around, locked it, and walked into the bar half out of breath.

I took a moment to compose myself while I strained my neck to locate everyone. When I didn't see anyone I went over to the bar and ordered a glass of wine. You always look less socially awkward when you have a drink in your hand.

So much for being late. I pulled out my phone and texted Grace. *You coming?*

She didn't respond. I took another sip of wine. It was only ten minutes after the meeting time. They'd show up.

Twenty minutes later my wine was gone, as was any of my motivation to wait around. My phone buzzed. *Sorry. We had to cancel, but someone else is coming.*

Someone else? My chest clenched. What was going on?

I promise you are going to love him. His name is Brad and he's been dying to meet you since he saw your picture.

What? You know I'm not interested in dating.

Of course I know. Why else would I make up a girls' night?

I silently cursed her before stuffing my phone back in my purse. Luckily I had a ten in my wallet, so I tossed down the cash and got up. Whoever this Brad was, I had no interest in meeting him.

I was never talking to Grace again. She may have been my last friend in town, but that didn't make up for this. We'd been friends since the first week of our freshman year of college, and she set me up with no warning? How pathetic did she think I was?

I hurried toward the entrance, carefully maneuvering through the crowd until I walked into something—or rather into someone.

"Sorry," I mumbled before I tried to walk around him.

"Ainsley?" A hand wrapped around my arm. I looked up at the sound of my name coming from a stranger's mouth. "Am I that late?"

I glanced into the deep brown eyes of a guy I'd never met. "Uh, sorry, you've got the wrong person." Was my luck really that bad? I literally ran into the blind date I was ditching.

"I'm Brad. Didn't Grace tell you about me?" He still held onto my arm a little too tight.

"Not until a minute ago."

"Wait. You didn't know we had a date? Didn't Grace show you my picture or anything? And why are you here then?" He glanced over my head as though someone else might somehow have the answers. The only one with the answers was Grace, and she was conveniently not there.

"I was supposed to be having drinks with friends."

"Oh." His eyes set on mine. "How about having drinks with me instead?" His lips twisted into a smile.

Talk about confidence. Too bad that wasn't going to change the fact that I was angry and in no mood to deal with him. "Sorry, I've got to go."

"Just one drink? I've been looking forward to this all week."

All week? Grace was really going to get it. We'd only planned the night out a few days ago. "There are plenty of girls here, I'm sure you'll find someone to occupy your time." I put a hand over my mouth. Had I just sounded that bitchy? He probably had no clue what he'd stepped into.

He laughed. "Feisty. Nice."

And any sympathy for him disappeared at the use of the word feisty. "Not feisty and not nice." I shook my arm, but it didn't budge from his grip. I swore I'd start working out with weights more. "Listen, I'm sorry if you're disappointed, but I never agreed to meet you."

"I get that, but why leave now? Might as well enjoy the evening, right?" He smiled.

I sighed. "Let go of my arm, and I'll think about agreeing to a rain check."

"A rain check?" He glanced at his watch. "But it's early. Why not have a drink now?"

"Because I'm annoyed, and nothing good is going to come of anything I do when I'm annoyed."

He laughed. "Fair enough. Can I get your number? Maybe set something up without involving Grace?"

"How about you give me yours, and I'll call you?"

He raised an eyebrow. "You mean so you can lose my number and never call?"

I crossed my arms over my chest. "You don't think I will?"

"I know you won't."

"Then why bother getting my number? I could blow you off that way too." I gazed longingly at the exit. It was so close yet so far away.

"No, you like being chased. I understand girls like you,

and I'm willing to play the game. Usually the reward is well worth the effort."

"Ok, offer to take your number revoked. Goodnight." I turned away. What an arrogant jerk.

He grabbed my arm again. "What? I'm just saying it like it is."

"Like it is? No, what it's like is that you're going to let go of me and walk away right now. Preferably forget my name."

I used his momentary shock to slip away. I made it to the door and stepped out into the cool night.

Holding on to my arm once was one thing, but twice? I'd done the whole Neanderthal guy thing before, and I wasn't interested in going there again. He'd turned out to be the biggest mistake of my life, and Brad was no different. He screamed alpha male asshole, and I didn't need that in my life. Boring was better than that.

I dared one glance over my shoulder before walking around the block to my car. At least I'd parked close. I tossed my phone on the passenger seat.

I spent two minutes getting my car out of the cramped spot, miraculously sparing my car and the others from any scratches. I drove home slowly, in no real rush to face the giant empty house. It wasn't my house.

A former professor had talked me into house sitting for one of his old friends. I didn't mind the rent free part, but there was something depressing about living alone in a giant house when you were single and nearly broke.

I marveled at the live oaks as I drove down the narrow streets. I loved Charleston, but there were some things about urban life I'd probably never get used to. The house came into view. It was gorgeous. Three floors and right near the battery.

It was so close to the water that you could nearly taste it, and you got an amazing view from the upper balconies. I had no trouble understanding why it was a stop on the historical tours, even if it did get annoying when people parked out front to take pictures.

I pulled around to the side of the house and parked in the small drive. When I got out, I did what I always did, I checked over my shoulder before walking up the wraparound porch. Living alone in a city wasn't good for an already paranoid person.

I unlocked the door and quickly locked it behind me. I glanced at the large kitchen. It was tastefully done, but I was surprised the owners hadn't updated it. Then again there was something charming about the old countertops. Granite might have taken away from the overall feel of the place.

The thought of a late night snack appealed, but a glass of wine sounded even better. I filled a tumbler two-thirds full with some left over Cab Sav. Although I was broke, there were certain luxuries I indulged in. I walked down the hall to the living room. At least there was a big screen TV to keep me company.

Forged in Stone is available now!

Want to stay up to date on Alyssa Rose Ivy's releases?
Join her mailing list: eepurl.com/ktlSj

Printed in Great Britain
by Amazon.co.uk, Ltd.,
Marston Gate.